POKÉMON™

Unova Region
A Legendary Truth

Pokémon
Unova Region
A Legendary Truth

Adapted by R. Shapiro

Scholastic Ltd

CHAPTER 1

"**W**ow! It's huge!" Ash said, craning his neck to look up at Dragonspiral Tower.

"*Pi-ka,*" Ash's Pokémon partner agreed from his shoulder.

Ash's friends Iris and Cilan were by his side, gazing up at the huge stone ruins in awe. Iris's Axew liked to hang out on her shoulder, just like Pikachu did with Ash. They'd all been traveling together on a journey to the White Ruins. Their friend Professor Cedric Juniper had discovered that the ruins might contain important data about the mysterious Light Stone and the Legendary Pokémon Reshiram. They couldn't wait to join him there!

Just then, they saw an SUV driving toward

them on the dirt road leading to the tower. A man with a beard and sunglasses waved from the car's window.

"Hey there, everyone!" he called. "Are you by any chance close friends of Professor Juniper?"

"We are, but why?" Ash asked.

"I happen to be Professor Cedric Juniper's assistant, and he's waiting for you at the White Ruins!" the man said. He'd come out to Dragonspiral Tower to pick them up.

Ash and his friends happily climbed into the SUV.

* * *

Little did they know that two lookouts in an armored vehicle were nearby, watching and listening to them. They were on Team Plasma, a mysterious group with an evil plan: to target and control Pokémon, with the ultimate goal of world domination.

When the two spies saw Ash and his friends drive off toward the White Ruins, they followed.

"Shall I contact Lord Ghetsis?" one asked the other.

"After N shows up," his companion responded.

* * *

And little did the Team Plasma spies know that *they*, too, were being watched and followed. Team Rocket—Ash's longtime rivals—had Team Plasma in their sights from a nearby hilltop. The two teams had recently clashed—they did *not* get along.

"So the White Ruins are about to have twerpish visitors," Jessie said.

"I couldn't care less about ruins . . . but the Light Stone is another story," James added.

"It looks like Team Plasma shares your enthusiasm," Jessie commented.

Their Pokémon companion, Meowth, was busy on his computer. He was pleased with how successfully the transmitter he'd planted was helping their spying.

"Soon, we'll grab Pikachu!" Jessie imagined.

"The Light Stone, too!" James added.

"I can't wait to stop Team Plasma," Meowth said. He held up his razor-sharp claws. "I can't wait to make noodles out of those goons!"

*　　*　　*

Soon, Ash and his friends had reached the White Ruins. Professor Juniper's assistant led them toward the excavation. They were below the forest in a shallow canyon that had a stone floor placed by an ancient civilization.

"Wow!" Ash said, looking around.

"This place is humongous!" Iris commented. Axew agreed.

"It's like tasting an ancient, exotic spice for the very first time!" Cilan said. He couldn't help describing his feelings about the place in food-related terms—after all, he owned a restaurant with his brothers in Striaton City.

They reached the excavation site. Ash, Iris, and Cilan were interested to see a number of Timburr, Conkeldurr, and Golurk hard at work. The strong Pokémon were lifting and moving heavy stones around the site.

"We never would have made it this far without their combined strength," Professor Juniper's assistant explained. "They're excellent excavators!"

Ash loved watching them work. "Wow," he said, "I wish N could see all this!" He was thinking of his friend N, whom he'd met on his earlier adventures in Unova. N was a sensitive soul and could hear the inner voices of Pokémon.

The professor's assistant drew Ash from his thoughts. "Let's move along! We may have made a monumental find—this way," he said, leading them toward an opening into the rock face. "We haven't fully excavated the entire site yet, but the White Ruins are by far the largest we've found to date!"

They walked down a long stone tunnel, passing many hallways branching off to the sides. When they turned down one, there were even more hallways branching off it, too.

"It feels like you could get totally lost in here," Iris said, glancing around.

"Axew!" her Pokémon agreed.

Finally, they reached Professor Juniper's workspace. He stood before what looked like a large doorway that was blocked up with a grid of square stones. Each stone had a symbol

carved into it. The professor studied his
notebook, his brow furrowed.

"Professor Juniper!" Ash called to him.

The professor faced them and cried, "No!
Stay put! Don't take another step!" Everyone
gasped in fright. ". . . If there were any danger,"
he finished cheekily.

Everyone groaned, remembering that the
professor always spoke very dramatically.

"I guess you still have a way with words,
Professor," Iris said with a chuckle.

He laughed heartily. "You haven't forgotten
rule one for adventurers, have you?" he asked.

"'Act after I finish my thought,'" Cilan replied. "How could we?"

"You're exactly right!" the professor agreed. "And thank you for coming all this way!"

"No, thank *you*!" Cilan replied.

Ash was eager to get moving. "So please, Professor, tell us about this great discovery!" he said.

Professor Juniper turned toward the doorway. "From what I can understand of the ancient hieroglyphs etched on this mural, behind that door lies a most important *something* related to the Legendary Pokémon Reshiram!"

"That's the Legendary Dragon-type said to control fire!" Iris said.

"And the legend says it generates flames from its tail that can burn through anything!" Cilan added.

Iris, Cilan, and Ash marveled at what the mysterious door might reveal. Learning more about Reshiram would be a monumental discovery indeed!

Professor Juniper was ready to try opening the door. The wall of stone blocks was like a giant puzzle with one piece missing. The professor slid one stone over to the right, then another downward, then another to the left, and another upward. He stood back . . . and a stone slid forward on its own to fill the missing space.

Then the symbols on the stones began to glow. The whole doorway blazed with bright blue light. When it faded, the stones had disappeared!

CHAPTER 2

The group walked through the empty doorway into an enormous round chamber with stairs leading downward. They descended to the bottom and looked around. Light was coming through a hole high up in the ceiling.

"Fascinating," Professor Juniper observed. "This seems to be the remains of a dormant volcano!"

The chamber held a circle of large stones, and in the center was a carved pedestal with a spherical rock on top of it. The rock was an unusual color—a shimmery swirl of purple and light green.

"What is that?" Ash asked.

"That's the Light Stone!" Professor Juniper said. Everyone gasped—then the professor

continued, ". . . Or, it's just a round rock."
Everyone groaned. He'd struck again!

But Ash was intrigued. "Do you know what the Light Stone is?" he asked Iris.

"Some say it's Reshiram transformed into another shape," Iris said.

Ash and Cilan were excited to hear that. "That means we could be seeing the actual Reshiram here, right in front of our eyes!" Cilan said.

"Perhaps," Professor Juniper replied as he approached the stone. "Let's get it out of

here for a closer look." He lifted it up, and light began to swirl from within it. Then it burst into magical flame! Tails of fire shot out in all directions, then came together in one powerful stream that snaked its way up into the air. It shot straight upward out of the hole in the ceiling in a huge blast.

From far away, outside the ruins, it looked like the volcano they were inside had come back to life! In fact, N could see it from a nearby hill. He was surprised to see the sudden stream of fire, but quickly understood what it was. "That's where you've been . . . Reshiram," he murmured.

N dismounted from the Sawsbuck he was riding. "Thank you for bringing me here," N said to it, rubbing its face. "It's dangerous from this point on—you should return to the forest."

Sawsbuck gave N a lick on the cheek to show that it understood.

N wasn't the only one who had seen the stream of fire. Elsewhere in the forest, a group from Team Plasma had been approaching the

White Ruins, and they were shocked by the sight.

"Analyze it, quickly!" commanded Barret, the group leader.

Back inside the volcano, Professor Juniper was still holding the stone. The stream of firelight ended, and his companions all ran over.

"Professor, you're not hurt, are you?" his assistant asked.

"No, I'm just fine," the professor said. "Since the stone's back to normal, let's go!"

The group came back out into the open air with the stone. "Okay, I'll go and get the analysis equipment," the professor's assistant said, heading off.

Professor Juniper set down the case he'd put the stone in and took it out.

"So, Professor, is this really the Light Stone?" Ash asked.

Professor Juniper was examining the stone with a jeweler's loupe on his eye. He said, "Well, although I can't be a hundred percent certain without a close analysis of the molecular

structure . . . No, this is *not* the Light Stone—"
Everyone gasped, surprised, until the
professor continued speaking. "—is something
I can't say for sure just yet." Everyone groaned.
He was too much!

But his information was still useful. "Hold on,"
Ash said.

"If he just told us there's no proof that it's *not*
the Light Stone . . ." Iris continued.

"Then that means there's a good chance it *is*
the Light Stone!" Cilan finished.

Nearby, Barret was spying on them from

behind a crumbling stone wall. A Team Plasma grunt approached him.

"Agent Barret, my analysis shows that that burst of energy was from the Light Stone," he reported.

"So it *is* real," Barret said, thoughtful. "Let's report this to Aldith and Lord Ghetsis right away!"

*   *   *

Ash asked Professor Juniper, "Okay, so if you've really got the Light Stone, how do you change it back into Reshiram?!"

"I don't know just yet," the professor replied. "But here's what the White Chapter of Pokémon Mythology has to say!" He set down the stone to explain the legend further. "When a person who is searching deeply for the truth seeks it, Reshiram will appear. At first, Reshiram will battle with that person as a test of their strength and heart. And if it decides that the person is a hero, it will pass on the wisdom it has accumulated over thousands of years and then bare its fangs against the hero's enemies."

Professor Juniper continued, "From that point on, Reshiram will treat the hero with kindness, as a parent would treat a child. But, although the person called the hero will be able to attain great riches and power . . . the goodness in their heart will be lost!"

"And the country built by the hero will be consumed in flame," another voice added. "Then, Reshiram will depart."

CHAPTER 3

Ash whipped around, looking for who had spoken. "What was that?!"

N was standing on a rise of stone above them. Ash and Pikachu were happy to see their friend—and Agent Barret was very interested to know he'd arrived.

"He's finally shown up," Barret reported over his headset to Aldith.

She was flying in a high-tech helicopter toward the White Ruins with Colress, a Pokémon researcher. "Understood," Aldith said to Barret. "Continue surveillance. We'll arrive on location in ten minutes."

Team Plasma's leader, Ghetsis, checked in with the helicopter via video call. He'd predicted that N would come.

"Lord Ghetsis, I promise you that *this* time, N will be secured!" Aldith said.

"He had better be," Ghetsis replied menacingly. "Oh, and Dr. Colress, what is the status of the completed device?"

Colress's eyes were in constant motion as he stared at the stream of numbers scrolling across the computer on his lap. "No problems whatsoever," he said to Ghetsis.

"So, when Reshiram appears, you know what to do," Ghetsis said.

"Yes, without a doubt," Colress agreed with a smug smile.

*　*　*

Ash asked N what he was doing at the White Ruins.

"I detected suspicious activity by Team Plasma," N said. "And I sensed the presence of Reshiram."

"Could be the Light Stone," Iris said. "It sounds like it to me!"

"Yes. It seemed rather sad," N agreed.

Professor Juniper looked up. "Who's this young man?" he asked.

"He's N and he's a friend of ours!" Ash said.

A friend? N thought. He considered Pokémon friends, but not often other humans.

N addressed Professor Juniper. "Professor, I'm aware of who you are. And I'd like to know what you're planning to do with the Light Stone."

"I'm going to take my time and investigate it

thoroughly!" the professor replied confidently.
"After all, Reshiram and the Light Stone are
part of my lifelong research."

"Oh, I see," N said, bowing his head. "Then
there's nothing else to say." He leaped down
more smoothly than seemed possible, grabbed
the container with the Light Stone in it, and
made another impossibly large leap away
from them.

Ash and his friends were shocked. "N, wait!
Why did you do that?" he called.

"Pika pika!" Pikachu was just as confused.

N turned back and declared, "I can't let Professor Juniper take this."

"Why can't you?" Iris asked.

"Because, long ago, I witnessed Reshiram destroy Team Plasma and then fly away!" N answered. He remembered that terrible, fiery day. He continued, "I've always wanted to ask Reshiram why. Why burn everything up like that? What was it so angry about? And what does it think of people? Reshiram is bigger than life itself to me . . . and if it's angry with people, I want to quiet that anger! I want all Pokémon to live in freedom. I want to know what is the truth and what it is that is wrong! I want Reshiram to show us the way."

"So why don't you work *with* Professor Juniper?" Ash asked.

"No!" N replied disdainfully. "He confirmed what I suspected. The Light Stone is just an object of scientific interest to him!"

"That's not true!" Professor Juniper protested. ". . . Or, maybe it is!" he added.

Iris was exasperated. "Will you save that kind of talk for another time, PLEASE?!" The professor was not helping the situation!

N said, "This is how it has to be." Then he ran away with the Light Stone.

"N! Hey, wait!" Ash called. He started running after him through the ruins. "N! Come back!"

N didn't slow down. "Ash, please! Just let it go! Give it up!" he said.

"But N, I want to talk to you more about all this!" Ash cried.

Suddenly, the ground crumbled underneath his feet! Ash tumbled into a hole.

N heard his scream and came back to help—but when he was a few feet away from Ash, the ground crumbled underneath him, too! They were trying to figure out their next move when the whole area caved in. A new passageway had been created—a deep hole leading far underground.

Iris and Cilan had caught up with Ash and N in time to see them fall, but they weren't close enough to help.

N had managed to grab the edge of the hole with one hand—the other hand still held the Light Stone. But Ash hadn't gotten a grip. He and Pikachu began slipping farther down among the falling debris. Only N could help them . . . but he'd have to drop the Light Stone to do it.

N took a deep breath, then dropped the stone and grabbed Ash's hand.

"Thank you, N!" Ash cried, holding on tight.

But N could hold them both with one hand for only so long. Soon, his hand slipped, and they dropped down, down, down!

Iris and Cilan reached the hole and looked

down in dismay. They couldn't even see where their friends had fallen!

Professor Juniper ran up and asked what had happened.

"They fell in!" Cilan cried.

"I'm going down there," Iris said, determined.

"You can't!" the professor said. "It's like a maze down there, and you'll only put yourself in danger. I'm sure they're both fine! Leave the exploration of the ruins to a pro like me."

Iris was worried but reluctantly agreed. "Please be safe!" she yelled down into the hole.

CHAPTER 4

"*ika, pi . . .*" Pikachu was worried about its best buddy. Ash was lying still on the ground! But then he opened his eyes and smiled at his Pokémon partner.

"Hey, Pikachu. Thank goodness you didn't get hurt!" he said. Then he sat up and realized where he was. "Hey, where's N?" he asked.

"I'm right here," N answered, walking over. They were in a large underground room with stone walls. The floor was covered in a deep layer of sand, with stone columns and other debris poking out of it. "Ash, are you hurt?"

"No, I'm fine," Ash replied. "Thanks for trying to save me!"

"Oh, please, I really didn't do anything," N said. "We were awfully lucky that the sand cushioned our fall." The Light Stone had landed nearby.

They seemed to have fallen into the room through a large hole in the wall, but now it was blocked by rocks.

N and Ash looked at each other. "Unfortunately, it doesn't look like there's any other way to get out of here," N said.

*   *   *

Aboveground, Iris, Cilan, and Professor Juniper heard a huge crash. As they were looking around to see what it was, a voice commanded, "Don't move!"

It was Team Plasma! Members of the group were jumping out from behind the ruins all around them, each with a Poké Ball in hand.

"We have the White Ruins completely surrounded!" Barret said. "Don't do anything stupid. We'll be taking the Light Stone with us."

"Impossible!" the professor responded. "We don't have it!"

But Barret was one step ahead. "We're aware that N took the Light Stone and then fell down into the ruins. Now step back!"

Iris, Cilan, and the professor did as Barret said.

*   *   *

Trapped in the cavern, Ash and N huddled together on the ground. The Light Stone was at their feet, glowing fiery orange like a campfire.

"I've been thinking a lot since I last saw you," N said. "Why do Pokémon love you as much as they do?"

"Love me?" Ash asked.

N continued, "I've been chasing after Team

Plasma for such a long time, and I've witnessed all kinds of relationships between people and Pokémon. People who treat Pokémon like part of the family, people who work side by side with Pokémon, and people who abandon their Pokémon . . . And unlike myself, Concordia and Anthea have never left their closed-off world. I wish they'd learn more about the outside."

Concordia and Anthea were N's otherworldly companions. Along with N, they had grown up with Team Plasma in isolation from society— until they'd recognized Ghetsis's true corrupt nature and escaped. Ash and his friends had helped them before, but Anthea and Concordia were still deeply distrustful of other people.

N reached out for Pikachu and held it up.

"Piii-ka!" Pikachu said happily.

N smiled, then sighed. "I want to know why Pokémon exist in our world in the first place. What are they trying to tell us?" Ash stared at the Light Stone, letting N continue his meditation. "Maybe there's a perfect place somewhere in the world—where people and Pokémon can live together in peace," N said. "But thinking of the Light Stone as nothing more than an object of scientific interest shows that people still think of Pokémon as creatures that only exist to serve their needs."

"Aw, come on," Ash protested. "All that 'making them serve us' stuff . . . I don't know about any of that! All I know is that my buddy Pikachu and all Pokémon are friends that I care a lot about!"

"*Pika pika!*" Pikachu agreed.

But N didn't seem convinced.

Ash continued. "Any time I've been sad or happy or really mad about something, Pokémon have always been there by my side through it all. And that's why I want to learn more and more about Pokémon. 'Cause they're my friends!"

"That's the reason?" N asked.

"If we learn as much as we can about Pokémon, then that will help us become better friends with them!" Ash replied. "So if it's true that Reshiram can be transformed from the Light Stone, I wanna become friends with it, too!"

N chuckled. "With Reshiram?!" He hadn't considered that possibility!

* * *

Up on the surface, Team Plasma was organizing their units, battling the excavation team's Pokémon, and getting their equipment ready. Aldith ordered Barret to assemble a group to retrieve the Light Stone from N, beneath the ruins.

Just as Barret was going to execute the orders . . .

"Don't move!" Professor Cedric's assistant grabbed Aldith and threatened her with a heavy pipe!

"Who are you?!" Barret was shocked at this turn of events.

"I wasn't planning to reveal my true identity until Ghetsis arrived, but I have no choice," the assistant said—then he pulled off a full-head mask to reveal an entirely different man underneath. "I'm Detective Looker of the International Police! And you're all under arrest!"

Iris and Cilan were thrilled by this turn of events!

Detective Looker quickly took control of the situation, moving Iris, Cilan, and Professor Juniper to safety as some of the excavation team's Golurk approached.

But Aldith wasn't worried. "Do you really think you can defeat a whole unit alone?!"

"Whenever I make a move, the whole International Police moves with me!" Looker said. "So, rest assured, backup is on the way!"

"Well, then I say they'd better hurry," came a chuckling voice. It was Colress, who'd just driven up to the edge of a cliff above the group in a high-tech vehicle. The front of it looked like a satellite dish.

What was that?! Looker recognized how dangerous it was. "No, it can't be!" he cried. "The Pokémon control device!"

CHAPTER 5

Colress activated the Pokémon control device. It shot out a blue beam of light that hit the Golurk. They crackled with blue energy . . . and then their eyes turned an evil red, and they started to go on a rampage against the excavation team they worked with!

Colress was extremely satisfied. "You should be grateful," he said. "You're witnessing firsthand the immense power of a device that will change the entire planet!"

"A device that completely takes over the mind of any Pokémon . . ." Looker was disturbed. "You've finally perfected it!"

"And that's not all!" Aldith said as she grabbed Barret. Then the two of them glowed

with green light and floated up to the Pokémon control device. "We can transform Pokémon into weapons!"

Looker realized that they'd used Telekinesis to ascend the cliff—Colress had forced the Golurk to use the move. Looker turned toward the mind-controlled Pokémon. "Sorry, Golurk! We're fighting back!"

Cilan tossed a Poké Ball and called, "You heard him, Crustle! Let's GO!"

At the same time, Iris tossed her Poké Ball and cried, "Dragonite, come on out!"

Crustle and Dragonite appeared in a flash. The Golurk immediately started attacking them, and Cilan and Iris directed their Pokémon to use Rock Slide and Flamethrower. Lights flashed, rocks fell, flame blasted, and smoke swirled.

Aldith ordered a nearby Team Plasma unit to help the Golurk fight, and Barret brought out Team Plasma's group of Liepard. Their moves blasted down, and Iris, Cilan, Looker, and the professor braced for their impact.

From a cliff above the action, Team Rocket was observing the battle.

"How long are we going to stand up here and watch?" asked James.

"Until Team Plasma gets its grubby hands on the Light Stone!" Meowth replied.

"Which we'll then grab for ourselves at the very last minute. And of course, Pikachu, too," Jessie added.

Meowth smirked. "Until that last minute, let's just sit back, relax, and watch the fireworks!"

*   *   *

Deep underground, it was silent in the cavern where Ash and N sat. Then N straightened up with a start. "Did you hear that?" he asked.

"Huh?" Ash didn't hear anything.

"Friends' voices . . . their shouts . . ." N said. "Could Team Plasma be the cause of this?"

Ash did not like the sound of that. "Come on, we've gotta get out of here!"

"Right," N agreed. "There has to be another way out. We've just got to find it!"

He and Ash both ran to explore the cavern again.

Team Plasma had organized a huge, coordinated attack. Their group of Liepard, along with a big group of Golurk, Conkeldurr, and Timburr—who were now under Team Plasma's control—were charging forward.

"This is too dangerous for my taste!" Cilan added.

Looker agreed. "We've got to keep them back at all costs!"

Iris and Cilan worked with their Pokémon to put up an amazing defense. Dragonite's Flamethrower hit the Liepard as Crustle's Rock Wrecker smashed into the Conkeldurr and Timburr. Then Cilan called for Rock Slide from Crustle, and Iris had Dragonite freeze the wall of rock into place with Ice Beam. Team Plasma's Pokémon were stopped in their tracks!

"Now's your chance to get out of here!" Looker said.

"Where do we escape *to*?" Iris asked.

Professor Juniper knew his way around.

"This way!" he cried, and he, Iris, and Cilan ran to hide.

Soon, though, Golurk, Timburr, and Conkeldurr punched their way through the icy rock wall, clearing the way to advance along with the Liepard. But Dragonite and Crustle weren't giving up—they kept attacking, making direct hits with Flamethrower and Rock Wrecker.

"So they're going to insist on getting in our way, eh?" Colress said as he watched the scene from above in the Pokémon control device. His fingers flew across his computer screen. He aimed the device's beam directly at Dragonite and Crustle.

Cilan, Iris, and Professor Juniper were watching from their hiding spot behind some of the ruins. The professor realized what was happening. "Oh no!" he cried. "They're attempting to control your Pokémon! Get them back in their Poké Balls!"

Iris and Cilan were shocked, but immediately pulled out their Poké Balls and called their Pokémon back in.

Dragonite and Crustle returned—just in time. The beam from the Pokémon control device hit empty ground.

"Yew! Axew-yew-yew!" Iris's buddy Axew cheered from her shoulder.

Iris gasped. "Stop! They'll try to control you, too!" she told Axew, hiding it under her hair.

Luckily, Team Plasma hadn't gained control of Iris's and Cilan's Pokémon—but the Pokémon also weren't able to fight them. The villains cheered, "There's no one to stop us now!"

Barret ordered all the Pokémon under their control to attack. With glowing red eyes, the many Conkeldurr, Timburr, and Golurk reared back and marched forward. Five Shadow Ball attacks from five Liepard blasted away the ruins that were hiding Cilan, Iris, and the professor.

They ran out of the smoking rubble—but ended up right in Team Plasma's grasp. "It's over!" one of Team Plasma's grunts announced.

Team Plasma bound up Professor Juniper, Iris, and Cilan in metal cuffs that secured their arms against their bodies. They were trapped, and there was nothing they could do.

CHAPTER 6

Detective Looker was hiding—he hadn't been caught by Team Plasma, but he was frustrated by not being able to help his friends more. "I know the International Police backup is on the way, but at this rate, Team Plasma could grab the Light Stone!" he muttered. "But even if I get out there now, I don't stand a chance." He didn't have any Pokémon—just the piece of pipe he was using as a weapon.

Team Rocket was also watching the action from the sidelines, but they were happy to be there. Jessie and James were getting ready to make an entrance and try to steal the Light Stone, but Meowth encouraged them to keep waiting. "Slow 'n' steady wins the race," he reminded them.

Meanwhile, Ash, Pikachu, and N were still trying to get back aboveground. They hadn't been able to find a passageway out of the cavern, so they'd started trying to dig their own tunnel out of the stone. It was exhausting work, and so far they'd made only a tiny dent in the wall.

Ash noticed N had stopped working. "N, what's wrong?" he asked. "Are you sensing things out there again?"

N shook his head, then bowed it with a somber look on his face. "I can't sense anything," he said. "I could hear their screams echoing loudly in my head, but now . . . everything's quiet."

Ash was worried, but then his optimism won out. "You know, N, Professor Cedric Juniper has taught us a whole lot of stuff! He has all these adventure rules," he said. N looked up, curious. Ash continued, "Adventure rule number four: You never give up until the very end! 'Cause there's always gotta be a way out. Get it?" He gave N a big grin. "I'm not giving up until the very end! So let's dig! And get out of here!"

Ash went back to chipping away at the stone, and Pikachu resumed digging with renewed energy. Soon, though, Pikachu's paws were too sore to keep it up. *"Pikaaa . . ."* it said sadly.

That made Ash realize his mistake. "Oh yeah! I forgot!" he said. He pulled out his five Poké Balls from his belt. "Let's get everybody to help us out!" He tossed them into the air, and one by one, Pokémon appeared in a flash. Oshawott, Pignite, Snivy, Krookodile, and Charizard—who let out a huge blast of flame.

"Okay, gang!" Ash said happily. "We wanna get out of here, so will you give us a hand?"

His Pokémon all cheered in agreement, and
then started discussing their plan of action.

Oshawott leaped up and sent a Hydro Pump
blast into the wall of dirt. N watched, amazed.

"Hey, great idea!" Ash said to Oshawott. "That
water will make the dirt a lot softer, so it's
easier to use Dig!"

When Oshawott finished, Krookodile stepped
forward and jumped straight into the dirt to
Dig. Next, Charizard used Dragon Tail, aiming
his swirling tail right into the tunnel Krookodile
was making. Then Pignite and Snivy came
over and helped move the dirt out of the way,
handful by handful. Pikachu used its tail to

scoop dirt, too. Ash cheered on each of his Pokémon as they made their moves. They made such a great team!

Oshawott held its paw up to Ash. *"Osha, oshawott!"*

"'Course I'll help, too. I'm coming!" Ash answered, hurrying over.

The team of friends kept it up, repeating the same moves to dig and dig.

N had been watching the action as if in a trance. "Incredible . . ." he said to himself. "Is that what it's like? The bond between Ash and his Pokémon?" He shook his head and ran over to help dig next to his friend.

*　*　*

On the surface, Aldith knew that her leader, Ghetsis, was soon approaching. She was anxious not to disappoint him.

"I've had enough! Force them to go underground, quickly!" she barked at Barret. "Hurry and secure N, and bring me the Light Stone!"

Barret jumped to action. "Golurk, use Shadow Ball and widen that hole!" he commanded.

The Golurk blasted their Shadow Balls directly at the hole where Ash and N had disappeared. As the smoke cleared, Team Plasma's Pokémon approached the hole to see if they could get down—right as Krookodile burst through the ground behind them!

The mind-controlled Pokémon and the Liepard stared the Intimidation Pokémon down, and it popped back down underground with a *"Krooookodile!"*

But it wasn't running away—it was just making space for Charizard, who burst out to the surface with a huge roar! The rest of

Ash's Pokémon jumped out behind Charizard, followed by Ash. He offered a hand to help N, who was climbing out with the Light Stone.

Though Iris, Cilan, Professor Juniper, and the excavation team were still locked up by Team Plasma, they were thrilled to see that their friends—and the Light Stone—were safe!

Ash and N looked around, taking in the situation. They noticed Team Plasma's leaders up on the rise above them. "So it *was* them, after all . . . ," N said.

Barret and Aldith also noticed the two young men. "Secure N and the Light Stone immediately!" Aldith ordered.

Barret commanded Liepard to use Shadow Ball at N.

N didn't move out of the way quickly enough—but Ash's Charizard jumped in front of N and took the attack's hit.

Then Golurk sent another Shadow Ball directly at Charizard, knocking it over!

Pignite did not like to see that. It ran over to its friend, worried. As another Shadow Ball attack came toward Charizard, Pignite sent a

Flamethrower back at it, blasting the attack away in midair. Then Charizard lifted its head up and talked with Pignite—Pignite seemed to be telling Charizard to not push itself so much. The Pokémon clearly cared about one another.

N watched the exchange and was astonished to observe their bond.

Ash called out, "Now, Pignite and Charizard . . . double Flamethrower!"

The two Pokémon each blasted the move, and the two streams of fire twisted together into an extremely powerful attack. It made a direct hit to Team Plasma's Pokémon, and Pignite and Charizard cheered.

Then Krookodile was ready to take a turn. To Ash's surprise, it spun around and started to use Dig. The huge cloud of dirt rained down directly onto Team Plasma's Pokémon! Ash praised the strength of Krookodile's Dig, and then saw that Oshawott and Snivy were asking to help, too.

"Sure! Oshawott, use Hydro Pump!" The stream of water smashed right into Team Plasma's Pokémon.

"Snivy, use Leaf Storm!" Ash called, and the swirling leaves made a direct hit as well. His whole team of Pokémon cheered for one another, and N watched in awe.

That strong bond isn't just between Ash and

his Pokémon, N thought. *When Ash is involved, an amazing bond forms among the Pokémon themselves!*

Barret was frustrated that the battle had not gone his way. But Team Plasma had its secret weapon. "Control those Pokémon, too!" Barret said to Colress, who was more than happy to oblige.

Professor Juniper, Cilan, and Iris could see what was about to happen. "Ash, quick! Get everyone back in their Poké Balls!" Iris called. "Hurry up or they'll be controlled!"

"Controlled?! Huh?" Ash was surprised, but quick to act. He took out two Poké Balls and called Charizard and Krookodile back. Colress's beam was locked on to the remaining Pokémon and he was just about to fire it, when . . .

"No, you don't!" Looker bellowed, running over to the Pokémon control device with his piece of pipe raised above his head. Before he could get to Colress, two Team Plasma grunts tackled him—but it was enough of a distraction for Ash to get Pignite, Oshawott, and Snivy safely back into their Poké Balls, too.

"We made it," he said with relief. "They're just fine. Can't control them now!" Then he saw Pikachu standing nearby.

"Pika?" Pikachu wasn't sure what was going on. But everyone else started to understand.

"What about Pikachu?" Iris cried.

Cilan gasped. "That's right—Pikachu doesn't like to go in its Poké Ball!"

Ash was scared. He ran over to try to save his best buddy. But just as he was lunging to reach Pikachu . . . Colress's beam hit it.

CHAPTER 7

Pikachu was surrounded by blue light. It was clearly trying to fight off the mind control, but the machine won out. Soon, Pikachu's eyes glowed an evil red.

Ash was shocked. Surely his best Pokémon pal couldn't be turned against him!

But Pikachu growled and crackled with electricity. It turned away from Ash—then fired a Thunderbolt right at Iris, Cilan, and Professor Juniper, who ran away as fast as they could, their arms still bound to their sides.

Even Team Rocket, watching from a distance, was stunned by this turn of events.

Ash couldn't bear to see Pikachu attacking his friends. He ran over and planted himself in front of the Mouse Pokémon, who was still glowing with electricity. "Pikachu, STOP!" he cried.

Colress smirked at Ash's action. "A foolish attempt," he said.

Pikachu was growling, but Ash wasn't giving up. "Hey, buddy . . . ," he said, smiling, and then walked slowly toward his Pokémon.

But Pikachu scowled and blasted Ash with a Thunderbolt. Ash screamed in pain as he was shocked with electricity.

N watched, worried. *Even the strong bond between Ash and Pikachu can't prevent this*, he thought.

Iris, Cilan, and Professor Juniper had taken refuge behind some rubble. They were scared for their friend.

"Stop! You're gonna hurt yourself, Ash!" Iris called.

Ash wasn't convinced. Once the attack ended, he stood up slowly, scorched and sore. "Come on, Pikachu, it's me," he said. "Don't you know me? Buddy?"

But Pikachu just clenched its teeth and growled, its eyes glowing red.

"It's all right—I promise," Ash said as he got even closer and knelt down by his Pokémon. Pikachu was crackling with electricity. When Ash put his hands on its cheeks, Pikachu attacked with another Thunderbolt, knocking Ash back.

"Ash! Oh no!" Iris cried.

Colress observed calmly. "Trying to undo my

control on your Pokémon is a complete waste of your energy," he said.

N had seen enough. "Stop it right now!" he called up to Team Plasma. "Do you want me to destroy the Light Stone?"

That caught their attention! N took the Light Stone out of its case and held it up. It swirled with fiery orange light. He continued, "This is what you want: the Light Stone. And me too. Undo Pikachu's mind control and we're both yours! But if you refuse me . . ."

"Aldith, what should we do?" Barret asked her.

"Getting the Light Stone is our primary objective," she said.

Barret called to N, "Fine! It's a deal! We'll turn off the EM wave that's controlling Pikachu. Now, bring the Light Stone up to us!"

Ash was lying stunned on the ground with Pikachu in his arms—though Pikachu's eyes glowed red. It was still under Team Plasma's control. Then, suddenly, the mind control ended, and Pikachu returned to itself.

Pikachu looked up at Ash, upset. Then it fainted onto Ash's chest.

N looked at Ash and Pikachu with affection. He said quietly, "I won't allow them to hurt you anymore. I've learned so much from you. Both of you."

But Professor Juniper wasn't happy with N's sacrifice. "No!" he cried. "You must not hand the Light Stone over to Team Plasma!"

Just then, a high-tech helicopter flew into sight. Ghetsis had arrived. Aldith and Barret bowed when he landed.

"Sir, we have secured the Light Stone. We've captured N as well," Aldith told him.

"Very good," Ghetsis said, pleased.

"We'll prepare for the ceremony right away," Aldith said. Ghetsis nodded in assent.

They set up on a special raised platform in the White Ruins. The fiery orange Light Stone was placed on a pedestal in the middle of a circle of unlit torches.

As Ghetsis faced the stone, everyone was

watching—Team Plasma, their Pokémon, and their prisoners.

Team Rocket snuck down to watch, too. They were preparing to jump in at the right moment.

Only Ash and Pikachu weren't there—they were still lying on the stone ground where they'd fallen. Slowly, they both woke up.

"Pika pi," Pikachu said affectionately.

"Pikachu, you're back!" Ash was so happy that his buddy was itself again. Then they remembered where they were and sat up to see what was happening.

Colress had the Pokémon control device aimed at the ceremony platform.

N was in a body cuff on the ground, but he called up to Ghetsis. "Do you really want to make the same mistake all over again?" he asked. "Remember back—all the horrible things that happened when you first summoned Reshiram!"

"That won't happen this time," Ghetsis said, smug. "Because we now have the Pokémon control device. I have no need for you anymore."

As Ghetsis approached the Light Stone, the ten torches encircling it each lit themselves. Ghetsis held up his Team Plasma scepter. The torch flames shot upward and connected into a fiery, spinning sun that blasted down onto the rock floor, leaving a circle of red light. The circle was soon surrounded by many more circles made of intricate patterns and symbols, all glowing red. Then the Light Stone shimmered with white energy.

"O Legendary Pokémon Reshiram!" Ghetsis said to it. "Come forth and ignite your flames and descend into our world once more!"

The Light Stone began to pulse with light.

N called out to it, "Don't do it, Reshiram! You mustn't appear! For your own good! You must remain in the shape of the Light Stone, no matter what!"

In the distance, Ash was startled to hear N. He jumped up to get closer.

Beams of white light were coming out of the Light Stone. Ghetsis raised the bottom of his scepter toward it, and it began floating up into the air.

"Team Plasma! Stop it, now!" Ash cried.

But it seemed to be too late to stop what had already begun.

CHAPTER 8

Suddenly, a thick fog rolled in. Two attacks blasted down from it, the first knocking away the guards around N, and the second breaking off his body cuff.

Cilan recognized the moves. "That's Psybeam and Magical Leaf!"

"It's Concordia and Anthea," Ash said. "They've come to rescue N!"

Iris was ready to make her own escape as well. "Axew!" she called to her Pokémon, who was hidden under her hair. "Think you can break this band?"

Axew immediately started pounding away at the metal band.

Meanwhile, from within the mysterious fog, Concordia and Anthea spoke to N with an echoey voice. "What exactly has happened to you?"

N stood up and tried to make them understand what he was fighting for. "Listen to me!" he said. "Team Plasma is trying to awaken Reshiram! If they're successful, the tragedy that occurred years ago will surely be repeated! Reshiram was filled with so much rage! I have to find out why. If not, we'll never be able to understand one another!"

Two members of Team Plasma rushed over, but N threw them off while still addressing his former companions. "Without understanding, people and Pokémon are doomed—doomed without a future! I want Reshiram to believe in humanity."

"N—return with us," Concordia said from the fog.

"We cannot afford to lose you," Anthea agreed.

N refused. "I will *not* run away!" he said. "If you really want Pokémon to be happy, then battle with us, side by side!"

Two pairs of eyes appeared in the fog. Ash recognized them as Concordia's and Anthea's Pokémon—Gardevoir and Gothitelle.

Aldith also noticed. She immediately told

Colress to fire the Pokémon control device at them, even though they were hidden by the fog.

Ash saw the beam hit the Pokémon. "Oh NO!" he cried.

"All right!" Aldith said. "Now use your powers in the service of Team Plasma!" she ordered.

Concordia and Anthea were confused and dismayed. They asked their Pokémon what was wrong . . . but both Pokémon just attacked, knocking the young women over. Gardevoir and Gothitelle had been transformed into Team Plasma's weapons.

Back on the platform, the ten torches blasted

fire into the air, which formed a glowing ball surrounding the Light Stone. It got bigger and bigger.

"Answer, Reshiram!" Ghetsis cried. "We are awaiting your momentous return to our world!"

As everyone watched, the Light Stone erupted in a huge flash, transforming into Reshiram. The huge, white Legendary Pokémon spread its wings in the air and let out a giant cry.

While their captors were distracted, Axew finally broke through Iris's band. "Thanks!" Iris said. "Now go and see if you can free Cilan, too!"

"Axewww!" it responded eagerly and leaped over to Cilan.

Reshiram landed on the stone ground right in front of N, who looked up at it, suddenly fearful.

But Ghetsis didn't seem afraid. "Reshiram! Welcome!" he said confidently. "I am Ghetsis. I have been anxiously awaiting your return!"

The Legendary Pokémon let out a furious cry. Ghetsis responded, "I expected you'd be angry. That doesn't matter! You shall be my weapon!" He pointed his staff at Reshiram as Colress aimed the Pokémon control device's beam— and then fired it.

Reshiram cried out in pain as it tried to shake off the device's hold. Blue sparks flashed around its body. But it was soon overtaken. Its eyes glowed red.

Colress smiled, satisfied. "Reshiram is now completely under our control," he boasted. "It's perfect! I'm incredible beyond words!"

Ghetsis was eager to harness the Vast White Pokémon's power. "Hear me, Reshiram," he said. "By order of Team Plasma, I command you to engulf those people in flames!"

Reshiram let out a blast of fire, and then

another. N blew toward Concordia and Anthea as Ash and Pikachu braced themselves against the wind. Members of Team Plasma tumbled through the air along with dust and debris.

"Run away, or you're finished!" Looker called to Iris and Cilan.

Meowth's tail caught fire and he sprinted around helplessly before jumping behind a bush to put it out. Jessie and James were bracing themselves behind a rock, impressed by Reshiram's power. "Imagine Reshiram on call twenty-four hours a day!" Jessie marveled.

Then Reshiram shot a Fusion Flare fireball

at a stone wall, blasting it apart. Members of Team Plasma and their Pokémon were blown into the distance by the force, but Ghetsis didn't even notice—he was just satisfied with his new weapon. "Incredible power!" he said to himself, looking up at Reshiram.

Jessie and James were *not* impressed with that kind of leadership. "How self-centered can you get?!" Jessie said.

"Ghetsis doesn't seem to care what happens to his team!" James added.

Nearby, Colress seemed as greedy as Ghetsis. He studied the readouts of Reshiram's power on his Pokémon control device computer screen. "These numbers are impressive indeed. But there's still more . . . Reshiram's potential is far, far greater than this," he said. Reshiram's eyes glowed red as it roared. "Yes, let's prove it! Use Fusion Flare!" Colress commanded.

Reshiram shot another fireball, sending several Golurk flying.

Luckily, Iris, Cilan, and Professor Juniper

ended up sheltered behind some rocks. They checked up on one another, and Cilan called out Crustle to cut through the professor's body cuff.

Still in his hiding spot, Ash had seen enough. "We've got to do something, Pikachu," he said. "My friends, the Pokémon . . . we've gotta rescue all of them!"

"Pika. Pikachu!" Pikachu agreed.

Just then, N, Concordia, and Anthea approached Ash—and so did Team Plasma's group of Liepard.

"Pikachu, use Thunderbolt!" Ash said, and Pikachu charged up and aimed the attack.

* * *

Team Rocket wasn't happy with how things were going. "If we don't do something, they'll steal the world from us!" Jessie said, her hands on her hips.

"We've gotta grab that machine and scram outta here!" Meowth agreed.

"Then our Team Rocket empire will become reality!" James said.

They looked at Ghetsis proudly surveying the devastation Reshiram had caused, and agreed that they'd never be okay with him as their boss.

Suddenly, an unfamiliar voice said, "You guys!" Team Rocket whipped around and realized who it was: Looker, of the International Police!

But Looker wasn't there to get them into trouble. "You're the only ones who can get us out of this awful mess," he said. "Help us out. Please!"

"Us, help *you*?!" James asked. "What for?"

But Meowth had a good reason. "For our rep!" he said.

Jessie agreed. "Team Rocket's time to shine!"

CHAPTER 9

While Ash and Pikachu were battling the Liepard, Barret called over the radio to Colress. "Aim the Pokémon control device at Pikachu!" he said.

Colress again locked Pikachu into the device's sights. Then Ash jumped in front of his Pokémon pal.

"No way!" he cried. "I'm gonna protect Pikachu no matter what!"

"That's foolish of you," Colress told him. "Sacrificing yourself for your friend won't do you any good." He locked the beam's sights back onto Pikachu, who was between Ash's feet.

Then Meowth's face filled his computer screen!

"Yo!" Meowth cried.

"Who is *that*?" Colress asked.

Ash was just as surprised to see his longtime rival helping him out.

Meowth extended his glowing claws. "You're gonna love this!" Meowth said, then slashed at the members of Team Plasma and Liepard around him with Fury Swipes. They ran away.

"Why are *you* helping us?" Ash asked Meowth.

"Don't sweat it," Meowth said. "Hide!" They ran behind a large stone, and Meowth said, "*This* twerp helper's gonna give you one shot." He pointed out Jessie and James with Looker

nearby. "We're all working together to destroy that device!"

"I gotcha," Ash replied. "Thanks for the help!" He offered to lure Team Plasma away from the Pokémon control device. "Pikachu, you stay here. If they see you, they'll try to control you."

Pikachu was sad to not be joining Ash. "Don't worry about a thing, buddy!" Ash said. "We're gonna protect you."

N, Concordia, and Anthea came out from hiding nearby, and Ash filled them in. "You should stay here and protect everybody!" he said to N.

"But how are you going to destroy the device?" N asked.

"It's being protected by a bunch of brainwashed Pokémon!" Meowth added.

"We'll just force our way in!" Ash answered.

Both Pikachu and Meowth weren't sure that was the best idea. Neither were N, Iris, or Looker, who all called for him to stop. It was too dangerous!

But Ash charged ahead.

Jessie and James had their own plan of attack.

"His job is little more than getting their attention," James said.

"While we're doing the heavy lifting!" Jessie added. "Let's go!" They ran off, to Looker's surprise.

"You're wasting your time!" Aldith called after all of them. "Our Pokémon will stop you!"

And just a moment later, Ash had to stop short, surrounded by all the Pokémon under the control of Team Plasma—Conkeldurr, Timburr, Golurk, Liepard, Gothitelle, and Gardevoir.

Pikachu couldn't leave its best pal alone in a situation like that. *"Pika pi!"*

As Pikachu ran out of its hiding spot, Meowth called, "Wait! You could get hurt!"

Ash saw it coming and said, "No, Pikachu!" But Pikachu kept sprinting, and Ash knew he couldn't change its mind. "Okay. If you're not gonna stay hidden, then use Quick Attack and move fast!"

As Pikachu blasted ahead with its move, N admired the connection Ash had with his

Pokémon. "Ash may not be able to hear a Pokémon's inner voice, but he sure understands their feelings," N said to Concordia and Anthea. "Isn't that the idea we've been searching for all this time?"

Up on the cliff, Colress had Pikachu in his sights again. He was just about to fire the Pokémon control device, but Pikachu dodged forward faster than he could follow.

Ash jumped backward as a Golurk stomped right where he'd just been. Then the Golurk cornered Ash, and Pikachu had landed too far away to help . . . but an attack hit Golurk right in

the back, knocking it away. It was Dragon Rage, from Iris's Axew!

"You just leave this to us, Ash!" Iris called from nearby.

But Iris and Axew were surprised by the group of Timburr and Conkeldurr that suddenly came over—and even more surprised by the moves that hit the Pokémon and stopped them from hurting Ash. They came from Team Rocket! It was a defense from Yamask, Woobat, and Meowth.

"We'll handle these jerks!" Jessie said.

"Long enough for you to give 'em the works!" James said.

"Make me proud of you, twerps!" Meowth said.

Iris and Axew cheered on Ash and Pikachu as they raced toward Team Plasma.

Ghetsis commanded Reshiram, "Get them!"

Coming face-to-face with the enormous Legendary Pokémon stopped Ash in his tracks. Then he came back to his senses. "Use Electro Ball and aim for the device!" he said to Pikachu.

Pikachu leaped forward and was in the middle of executing its move when Colress hit it with the beam from the Pokémon control device. It knocked Pikachu out of the air.

Ash ran toward his Pokémon, but he was

thrown backward in a blaze of electricity. N caught him.

Then they realized what was happening. "Amazing! Pikachu is fighting the device—fighting off the evil and trying to maintain control!" N said. Pikachu was alternately crackling with lightning as itself and glowing blue with mind-controlled red eyes.

Iris and Cilan ran over to help encourage Pikachu. Ash said to his Pokémon, "Pikachu, you can't let the device beat you! You can win this. I know you can!"

Colress thought they were being ridiculous. "My, my, you really like to dream, don't you?" he said. "My device is able to control the likes of Reshiram! What hope does your little Pikachu have of resisting it?"

Pikachu walked toward Reshiram, eyes blazing red but also crackling with lightning.

"Impossible!" Colress said. "There's no way you can resist!" But Pikachu was resisting, acting against what Colress had programmed.

"*Pi . . . ka . . . chuuuuu!*" Pikachu's

Thunderbolt burst upward, surrounding Reshiram. It screamed in the blast.

N said, "I can hear its voice . . . Reshiram's consciousness has returned. I sense great pain!"

Ash and his friends watched the Pokémon in shock as it seemed to struggle within the Thunderbolt's electric charge.

"It's trying to use Pikachu's Thunderbolt to escape the device's control!" Cilan realized.

Ghetsis was not happy. He approached Colress. "What is the meaning of this?!" he cried. "Raise the output! You must take control of Pikachu!"

Colress again hit Pikachu with the device's beam. Pikachu's eyes glowed red and it marched stiffly forward. But Ash and his friends were still on Pikachu's side.

"Don't give up, Pikachu!" Ash called.

"You've got to stay strong!" Iris cried.

Pikachu was still fighting hard against the device's control. It again tried to shake it off with a massive Thunderbolt.

"Pikachu, can you hear my voice?" Ash called. "Destroy the device! Use Electro Ball!"

Though its eyes were still glowing red, Pikachu heard him. It fired off Electro Ball. Reshiram also heard, and at the same time, it sent a Fusion Flare. The two attacks hit the Pokémon control device one after the other. It exploded in a burst of smoke.

All the Pokémon that had been under the device's control suddenly came back to themselves. The red glow left their eyes, and they looked around cautiously. They no longer had to fight against their will or against their friends.

"The twerps did it!" James cried.

"Pikachu's simply incredible!" Jessie said.

"Don't forget, teamwork led this race!" Meowth added.

N seemed shocked. "Does that mean we won?"

Pikachu slowly opened its eyes, then leaped into Ash's arms as he ran over.

"You were awesome, Pikachu!" Ash said, giving his best pal a big hug. Iris, Cilan, and the

rest of Ash's friends were thrilled at Pikachu's success.

Colress was looking down at the broken Pokémon control device in shock. "I can't believe it . . . it can't be true!" he said.

"I guess it's something you'll never understand," N said to him. "Nothing's stronger than the trust between Ash and his Pokémon!"

But Colress didn't listen. "My theories are indisputable. I won't quit!" he declared.

Reshiram gave a loud cry as it hovered in the air above them. Ash wondered what it was going to do next.

N looked up at Reshiram. "That voice . . .

the fierce voice of rage!" he said, sensing the Legendary Pokémon's feelings.

Though Colress's control device was broken, he could still see information about Pokémon on his computer. He was amazed at what he was seeing. "Incredible! Reshiram's power is far greater now than when I was controlling it," he said. "How can that be?!"

Reshiram roared and let out an enormous blast of blue fire. It pummeled the ruins, exploding Ghetsis's helicopter. Flames and thick smoke blew past as everyone braced against the flying debris.

Reshiram roared again. If it kept attacking, it would destroy the entire area!

N called out to the Pokémon, "Reshiram! Please try to control your anger!"

"You've gotta listen to us!" Ash added.

N continued, "We're not your enemies. People and Pokémon *can* live peacefully together." Reshiram stopped its cry and turned to look at N, who stepped closer to it, keeping eye contact. "You must know our feelings," he said. "How we truly care about you deep within our hearts. And that feeling will always be there!"

Reshiram seemed to understand, and it became less angry.

Ghetsis, however, was still angry. "Reshiram, this is unacceptable!" he yelled.

But Aldith and Barret knew they were beaten. They grabbed Ghetsis to pull him back.

"We must retreat!" Barret said.

Looker wasn't going to let that happen. "Don't let them escape!" he cried.

Ash was ready to help. He tossed a Poké Ball, calling, "Krookodile—Stone Edge!"

Cilan ordered Rock Slide from Crustle, and Iris tossed a Poké Ball to call Dragonite to use Ice Beam. Soon, the Team Plasma leaders were trapped, surrounded by giant boulders and encased in ice. The Pokémon high-fived one another as their Trainers praised their work.

Reshiram let out another roar. It wasn't angry this time—it was ready to leave.

But N called out, "Reshiram, wait!" He looked up at the Legendary Pokémon in the air, and it studied him.

"I've always wanted to meet you," N continued. "The last time I saw you, all I could feel from your heart was rage and anger. And

even now, I can sense your anger. I have to know something. You saw the way we joined together and battled evil here at these ruins— people and Pokémon alike. How did you feel when you witnessed that?"

Reshiram lowered its head slightly, locking its gaze with N's and communicating its feelings.

After a moment, N said, "I see. Thanks so much! The way we believe in Pokémon . . . I'm wondering if you could believe in people in the same way. Just like you, I'll keep fighting for the ideal world that all of us can live in!"

Reshiram reared back and roared, then

turned and soared off into the sunlight streaming down from the clouds.

Iris walked over. "When Reshiram answered your question, what did it say?" she asked N.

"Well . . . how can I put it . . ." N tried to find the words.

"You don't have to tell us right now!" Ash said—to the surprise of Iris, Cilan, and Pikachu, who were very curious.

"Why is that?" N asked.

Ash answered, "'Cause if I ever meet Reshiram again, I want to ask for myself! That'll give us something to look forward to, right?"

"Piii-kachu!" Pikachu agreed.

N approached his former companions. "Concordia, Anthea: Don't you think you've seen a lot of things that you could never have seen from within the fog?" he said. "From now on, stay with me. Let's travel out here in the sun!"

"But travel to where?" Concordia asked.

"To the ideal. To work toward turning that ideal into a reality!" N said. "But to do that, I need you both to help me."

The women both smiled in agreement. They were ready to join their friend.

Suddenly, the sound of sirens rang through

the ruins. The International Police had finally made it! Ghetsis, Colress, Aldith, and Barret were loaded into a van and taken into custody.

"Thank you, Ash," Looker said, getting into his police car. "I wouldn't have been successful without your help! We'll meet again!"

Ash waved as he drove off. "Take care of yourself, Detective Looker!"

Professor Cedric Juniper, however, was less happy with how the situation had turned out. "This is terrible!" he cried, wrenching his hair. "The Light Stone was a historic discovery!"

Then two of his assistants ran over. They'd just heard of some new ruins to go explore! The professor was immediately excited to go help with this new excavation. He called to his team to pack up. "We won't be meeting again," he said to Ash, Iris, and Cilan. ". . . Until we do!"

The three friends rolled their eyes.

* * *

Meanwhile, Team Rocket was running off into the sunset.

"So catching Pikachu is completely worth the effort after all!" James said. That Pokémon continued to prove its worth!

"Not to mention taking care of that annoying Team Plasma," Jessie said.

Jessie, James, and Meowth all gave a cheer for Team Rocket. They were feeling great!

*   *   *

N was ready to leave. He, Concordia, and Anthea had come over to say good-bye to Ash, Iris, and Cilan. "Thank you," he said. "It's now the right time for the three of us to take up this journey together—to create an ideal world for people and Pokémon."

"Great!" Ash said. He was happy for his friend to pursue his dream.

He was also happy with how this journey had turned out. They'd stopped Team Plasma, and it had been an amazing experience meeting the Legendary Pokémon Reshiram. Now Ash was ready for his next adventure!

Kalos Region
The Secret of Zygarde

Adapted by Jeanette Lane

Scholastic Ltd

First published in the UK by Scholastic, 2021
Euston House, 24 Eversholt Street, London, NW1 1DB
Scholastic Ireland, 89E Lagan Road, Dublin Industrial Estate,
Glasnevin, Dublin, D11 HP5F

SCHOLASTIC and associated logos are trademarks and/or
registered trademarks of Scholastic Inc.

First published in the US by Scholastic Inc., 2021

©2021 Pokémon. © 1997–2015 Nintendo, Creatures, GAME FREAK,
TV Tokyo, ShoPro, JR Kikaku. TM, ® Nintendo.

ISBN 978 1338 74654 9

A CIP catalogue record for this book is available from the British Library.

Printed by CPI Group (UK) Ltd, Croydon CR0 4YY
Paper made from wood grown in sustainable forests and
other controlled sources.

4 6 8 10 9 7 5 3

This is a work of fiction. Names, characters, places incidents and
dialogues are products of the author's imagination or are used fictitiously.
Any resemblance to actual people, living or dead, events or locales is
entirely coincidental.

The publisher does not have any control over and does not assume any
responsibility for author or third-party websites or their content.

www.scholastic.co.uk

CHAPTER 1

The Kalos League championship had just
ended, but Ash and Alain were running
for their lives. Outside Lumiose Stadium,
the city had turned into rubble. Thick vines
had pierced through the earth and snaked
around everything. The vines were laced with
blood-red veins, and they slithered across the

streets, wrapping around lampposts, cars, and buildings. The sky had turned a haunting red. Ash wondered how so much could have changed in such a short time.

The largest city in all of Kalos, Lumiose was known as the City of Light. When Ash and his team of loyal Pokémon first arrived, Ash had marveled at the many plazas filled with fountains and flowers. There were charming old buildings with romantic stone arches. The hotels and cafés were full of people. The streets were laid out in a circular pattern and lined with lush trees.

At the center of it all was the Prism Tower—a glowing beacon against the crystal-blue sky. Prism Tower was home of the Lumiose Gym, which specialized in Electric-type Pokémon.

Ash was thrilled when he had advanced to the Kalos League finals and learned he would compete against the dedicated Trainer Alain. Alain had started his own Pokémon journey with Professor Sycamore, right there in Lumiose.

One of Ash's goals in joining the Kalos

competition was to learn more about Mega Evolution, which was a fascinating new transformation that certain Pokémon could undergo. The transformation was temporary, so it lasted only a short time. In addition, it required the Pokémon to have a special Mega Stone, and the Trainer needed a Key Stone. Professor Sycamore believed that Mega Evolution was only possible if the Trainer and the Pokémon truly believed in each other. There was still so much they didn't know about Mega Evolution, but they did know it was stupendously powerful!

But now, giant vines had erupted all over the city. Ash knew something was terribly wrong.

Ash's friends spread out all over Lumiose, and everyone was on a mission. Ash agreed to help Alain, who wanted to track down Mairin, his friend and fellow Trainer. Clemont, the Lumiose Gym Leader, was with Bonnie, who wanted to find Squishy—the mysterious, tiny Pokémon whom she'd befriended after it had appeared in her bag during the group's travels. But Squishy had just run off, and Bonnie was distraught.

There was confusion everywhere as people and Pokémon scrambled to safety.

In a flurry of zaps and blasts, Ash realized he was under attack! Team Flare swarmed around Ash and dragged him off to meet with Lysandre, the head of Lysandre Labs.

*   *   *

Meanwhile, Lysandre introduced himself to all of Lumiose in a grand video announcement. His face and flamelike mane of hair were on every screen across the great city. His deep voice sounded calm, but his message was one of hatred and destruction.

"To my beloved Kalos region and the entire world: I am Lysandre. Team Flare is here with me to do my bidding. We are here to remake the world into a place of pure beauty and peace. Yes, Team Flare's purpose is to transform our world into an exquisite example of creation!"

The screen flickered to show a Pokémon on top of Prism Tower. Lysandre called it Zygarde. It had a large, flattened, legless body. A frill fanned out behind its head, like a crown. Zygarde looked regal and powerful.

"As leaders of this new order, Team Flare and I have decided to join forces with this powerful guardian of creation. Zygarde is angry at the

behavior of both people and Pokémon. The discipline of this world has been lost. Humanity is out of control. We have forgotten how to share!"

People all over Kalos watched Lysandre on televisions, computer screens, and phones. They were confused and frightened by his harsh declaration, his claim that the world was lost. Lysandre insisted that not sharing led to people stealing, and that there was not enough for everyone. He said the only solution was to reduce the number of people on the planet, and he claimed the Legendary Pokémon Zygarde was on his side.

"Only the chosen ones will move into our bright, hopeful future! We of Team Flare, along with the fury of Zygarde, will be the ones who will make the judgment. The new order will do away with the chaos of the world and bring about the beautiful world we desire!"

All around, people reacted with fear and uncertainty. Who was this man, and what did he mean by a "judgment"? Was he really going to decide who would—and who wouldn't—be part of a new world?

That was just the beginning of a long battle.

*   *   *

When Ash woke up from being captured, he was up in the air, high above Prism Tower. He was suspended hundreds of feet above the ground, restrained by electronic cuffs. Greninja, Pikachu, and his other Pokémon were in shackles, too, floating by his side. Below, Ash could see Lysandre and Alain standing on the roof deck of the tower.

Down in the streets of the city, Ash's friends

were waging battles of their own. The mysterious hero Blaziken Mask and his loyal Mega Blaziken joined up with Clemont, Serena, and Bonnie. Blaziken Mask wanted to escort them all home so they would be safe, but they refused. Clemont did not want to abandon Lumiose Gym, and Bonnie wouldn't rest until she found Squishy.

It wasn't long before Team Flare blocked them in front of Prism Tower, home of Lumiose Gym.

While they were figuring out what to do next, Bonnie suddenly could sense that her dear friend Squishy was near—and something big was about to happen.

It all started with a high ringing sound. Then there was a flash of neon green light, and Squishy appeared on the roof of a car, then on the side of a building. A brilliant green light glowed all around it, but Squishy stayed in one place for only a second before it disappeared and reappeared somewhere else.

The ringing sound grew louder, and a ball of light rose in the air. The sound seemed to vibrate with the bright green light until the light began to take shape. A head began to form, and a tail. The green globe floated into the sky, zipping here and there. It grew larger and longer—a skeleton of neon green light. Finally, the light dimmed and a black-and-green body with a majestic frill around its head appeared.

Squishy had fully transformed. It let out a roar.

"Squishy, yay!" Bonnie cried.

"That's unbelievable," Clemont said.

The scientists of Team Flare were just as surprised. Now there was another Zygarde! Team Flare believed that this had to be a good sign for them, and for Lysandre's vision for a new world.

CHAPTER 2

"Yes," Lysandre yelled from high on Prism Tower. "Zygarde is the Legendary Pokémon who watches over the world and punishes those who dare to disrupt its order. It is time for this world to start over again!"

Ash tried to make sense of it all. Below, there were now not just one, but *two* Zygarde in 50% Forme, and they were facing off. One was black and red. The other was black and green—the same green as Bonnie's beloved Squishy. Was Squishy really a Legendary Zygarde? Even though he had seen it transform, Ash could hardly believe it. Now Ash understood why Team Flare had been tracking Squishy. They knew its potential power!

The red Zygarde was full of anger and wreaking havoc. Ash realized Team Flare must

have control of it. But how had Lysandre and Team Flare taken over the Legendary Pokémon and fueled it with such anger?

The two Zygardes were preparing for battle. Would the Squishy Zygarde be able to stop Team Flare's Zygarde?

The two giant Order Pokémon reared up, screeching and emitting low, rumbling growls.

"Soon enough, this new Zygarde will come around to Team Flare's way of thinking. Then it, too, will turn red with rage!" Lysandre stated, sure of himself.

"No, you're wrong!" Ash insisted. "Squishy would never think like that!" Ash thought back

to how Bonnie first met Squishy, and how the tiny Pokémon had traveled with them as their trusted friend.

Ash turned to Alain. "What's going on with all this, Alain? Say something!"

*   *   *

While Clemont and the others battled the scientists from Team Flare, Bonnie was doing her best to appeal to both Squishy and the other Zygarde. It appeared that the green Squishy Zygarde was trying to communicate with the red Zygarde using telepathy, but no one could understand what it might be saying. No matter what the green Zygarde did, the red Zygarde stayed under Team Flare's control. Vines continued to grow all around the city as the two Zygardes hissed at each other and the sky crackled with bolts of red energy. Almost all the people had fled, trying to find safety.

"Oh, Squishy!" Bonnie cried. She would do anything to help Squishy, but she couldn't even tell if it could hear her.

The Zygarde reared their massive heads and exchanged spine-chilling mechanical screeches. All at once, the green Zygarde lashed out, barreling forward. It slammed the red Zygarde into a row of buildings with a crash. A cloud of dust filled the air.

"Squishy, no!" Bonnie yelled. She knew that Squishy would want to stop the evil plans of Lysandre and Team Flare, but she didn't want to see more destruction. "Squishy," Bonnie repeated, hoping her friend could sense her support. Then, she turned to look at the red Zygarde. "Please, Zygarde, listen to what Squishy's telling you. Please!"

Nearby, while Clemont, Serena, and Blaziken Mask were still exchanging attacks with Team Flare, two friends joined their crew.

"Professor Sycamore! Mairin!" Serena called out with relief.

Clemont was happy to know his friends were safe. But he knew that he had to take back Prism Tower and the Lumiose Gym in order to stop Team Flare's control of the city. Clembot, as always, was close by Clemont's side, and Clemont was going all-out, battling with Luxray, Chespin, Bunnelby, and more of his trusted Pokémon. Attacks of Wild Charge, Pin Missile, and Mud Shot blasted at Team Flare.

"Use Flamethrower!" Blaziken Mask directed. With a thrust of its talons, Mega Blaziken shot a wave of fire at their opponents.

The pesky Team Flare scientists were not giving up without a fight. Team Flare battled with Druddigon and Liepard. The Liepard prowled along the top of the rubble and blasted the young Trainers' Pokémon with Shadow Claw and Dark Pulse.

While the battle raged on, Serena went to
see if Mairin was okay. "Have you seen Alain
or Ash?" Mairin asked. "They said they were
coming to Prism Tower."

"No, I haven't seen them yet," Serena confessed.
"But you know you don't have to worry about Alain
and Ash. They are both strong!"

Mairin nodded, but her body shivered with
concern. "I'm still so worried about Chespie, too."

Serena took a deep breath. Chespie was the
nickname of Mairin's first Pokémon, a Chespin.
Professor Sycamore had given her Chespie when
she first started on her Pokémon journey. Serena
knew that Mairin's Chespie had not woken up for

some time. It had been in a deep sleep that no one understood. Serena also remembered that Mairin had trusted the scientists at Lysandre Labs to look after the sleeping Chespie, to help learn what was wrong—but they had just discovered that those same scientists were members of the evil Team Flare. Mairin had reason to be concerned. Chespie might be in danger!

"Mairin? Chespie's still at Lysandre Labs, right?" Serena asked, reaching out for her friend's hand.

"Right," Mairin said.

"Clemont?" Serena called.

Even though he was engaged in battle, Clemont understood exactly what Serena was asking. She wanted to get Chespie out of Lysandre Labs!

"Of course you should go!" Clemont called to her. "Don't worry, we can handle everything around here. Take care of Mairin and Chespie!" Clemont was determined to gain access to his old gym, but he would have to beat Team Flare first.

"Mairin, let's go," Serena said. "Chespie needs us!"

Professor Sycamore agreed to go with them. Lysandre Labs was all the way on the other side of the city, and the streets were full of danger.

Team Flare's Liepard zapped a purple pulse directly at Professor Sycamore's feet. "Blaziken Mask, take care of this!" the professor called out as he darted away.

Not far away, the two Zygarde were still lashing out at each other. Blooming clouds of dust and smoke rose all over the city. The Legendary Pokémon left a path of destruction with every attack.

"Squishy," Bonnie whispered, believing that her friend could hear her. "Squishy, I hope the other Zygarde listens to your heart."

CHAPTER 3

High above, Lysandre was still going on and on about his plans for the end of the world and the start of a new, better one. Ash and his Pokémon were still trapped in the floating cuffs. And Alain was still there, not quite believing what was happening.

"Alain, this is all thanks to you," Lysandre declared. "Mega Evolution gives us power. The power to control Zygarde."

Ash could see the shock on Alain's face.

"The Mega Evolution energy you gathered when you battled with Mega Charizard is proving to be quite useful in destroying this imperfect world. Just look."

Alain clenched his fists and shut his eyes. He shook his head. "But Mairin! Chespie! Is this

the reason I had all those battles? FOR THIS?"
The city was covered in slithering vines. The
roads were torn up, nothing but rubble. A dark
red cloud lingered over the city. Alain began
to weep.

"You did it all for Chespie's sake. For Mairin's
sake," Lysandre said, his voice dripping with
false sympathy. "Your wish had pure intent. A
truly noble wish, indeed."

Suddenly, Ash thought he understood. Alain
did not share Lysandre's evil vision. Alain had
worked with Lysandre only in hopes of helping
his friend Mairin, who had been worried about
her Chespie for so long. It had all started
during a visit to Lysandre Labs, around the time
that Bonnie had found Squishy.

"That's why Alain did this," Ash whispered to

himself. Ash hoped that Alain was starting to put it together, too. Had Alain figured out that Lysandre had used him? Lysandre had used Alain *and* Mega Charizard X so he could gain power from their Mega Evolution energy. Lysandre had claimed it would help Mairin's Chespie. But it was obvious that Lysandre would betray anyone in order to get the power he needed to conquer the world.

"So, Ash," Lysandre said, looking up toward his prisoner. "I'm going to use your Bond Phenomenon in service to my new world as well. You're able to gain the powerful strength of Mega Evolution without a Key Stone! You can do it purely through your bond! When I saw that, I was thrilled!" A devious smile stretched across Lysandre's face. "Ash, you have shown me that there are limitless possibilities with Pokémon. Still! And I want that power for myself!"

Ash was horrified! Lysandre did not understand anything about how Bond Phenomenon worked. He saw Pokémon only as a source of power. What Ash and Greninja shared with Bond Phenomenon *was* powerful, but its source was something stronger than anything Lysandre could comprehend. It was all about trust.

Just then, two small buzzing droids appeared from behind Lysandre. They had flapping wings, and they zipped up to Ash and Greninja. Once they were in position, a glaring red light burst from their mechanical heads. The hot light encircled Ash and Greninja, and the buzzing sound grew louder. Ash screamed as the blazing light burned deep inside him. Greninja grunted in pain.

"The energy from this light is powerful enough to control Zygarde. But now, Ash! Now, Greninja! I'm also going to control your Bond Phenomenon! I'm going to control you!" Lysandre exclaimed as he watched the light surround the young Trainer and his devoted Pokémon.

"No way," Ash insisted, willing himself to stay strong.

"From this point on, both of you will answer to me!" Lysandre yelled.

Pikachu, Noivern, Talonflame, and the others on Ash's team couldn't watch.

"Pika, pika," Pikachu worried out loud. It was more than the Electric-type Pokémon could take!

"Lysandre, please stop this!" Alain called, finally speaking up.

"There's no way you are ever gonna control the two of us!" Ash grunted through clenched teeth.

"You still don't understand, do you, Ash?" Lysandre said. "When the current world is a

thing of the past, you two will be the chosen ones who will guide all of humanity!"

"We're never gonna do any of that! We're never going to change," Ash asserted. Then he turned to his friend. "Alain, I don't know what happened to you, but you've got to stop all this. Now! I believe in the Alain I know!"

Ash's words seemed to snap Alain back to himself.

Ash continued, "I really care about this world! I care about the people and the Pokémon who call it home, and you won't destroy it!" Anger boiled inside him. He hated what Lysandre had done to Alain. But even more, he hated how Lysandre was using the Zygarde to destroy the world—and how Lysandre thought he could do the same thing with Ash and Greninja!

"Battle me, Lysandre!" Ash announced, his voice coming from deep in his gut. Suddenly, a blue-white beam of light appeared and reached straight up to the sky. The light spun around and around, like a whirlwind. The blue-white

light canceled out the red light of the flying droids. Ash screamed as the force of the swirling light spun around him and Greninja. The blue light grew brighter. When at last it burst, Ash and Greninja were no longer in cuffs. They were free! They landed on the roof of Prism Tower with a thud, and Greninja was in its Ash-Greninja form—with red stripes on its cheeks, stronger legs, and the ability to make Water Shurikens on its back.

Alain bent down to help Ash up. "Because of you," he said, "my head is clear. We've got to stop this. Together."

"Awesome," Ash responded, feeling renewed hope. "Now you're talking."

"Charizard," Alain called. "Use Dragon Claw to free Pikachu and the rest!"

"Pikaaa!" Pikachu was excited to be free— and to see Alain and Ash ready to battle together.

CHAPTER 4

"**S**quishy!" Bonnie cried. The two Legendary Pokémon were still trading attacks. The green Zygarde could not do anything to break Team Flare's control over the red Zygarde.

Just then, a powerful red ray shot out from Prism Tower. It came from Lumiose Gym. The ray burned with the same intense light that Lysandre had used to try to control Ash and Greninja. The ray streaked across the city, straight at the green Zygarde. Bonnie was right in its path! Luckily, Blaziken Mask swooped down and carried her away at the last second.

"Young lady!" Blaziken Mask shouted. "Why were you there all alone?"

"I'm scared Squishy's . . ." Bonnie stumbled

over her words. "I am scared Squishy is going to lose." Bonnie crumpled over, crying. Then she sensed something was terribly wrong. "Noooo! What's happened to my Squishy?" she cried. She knew Squishy was not the same.

A horrible laugh erupted from inside Lumiose Gym. Xerosic, one of Team Flare's scientists, turned off the switch to the gigantic machine, knowing its evil red ray had reached its target. "True success!" he announced. Then he informed Lysandre that Squishy Zygarde was now under their control as well.

It was true. Bonnie could feel it in her heart,

but anyone could tell by looking. Squishy Zygarde had changed from green to red.

Up on the tower, Lysandre broke into a devious laugh. "My world of peace will be created much faster now," he said, glaring at Ash and Alain.

"How can you say peace has anything to do with this?" asked Ash.

"What would you know about peace?" Lysandre answered. With that, a jetpack zoomed in and landed on his back, and the small flying droids attached to it with thick wires. Two weaponized arm bands wrapped around his wrists, and red goggles shielded his

eyes. He was in full battle mode. "You don't have a clue when it comes to the ugly parts of the world. There was once a time when I reached out to help people. People who were in need and suffering . . ."

Ash and Alain listened, uncertain.

"And they rejoiced. But that didn't last long! They all began to take my help for granted, and my help actually brought about their own arrogance. They were foolish, arrogant people." Lysandre's voice was full of disgust and hate. He went on to explain how the people came to depend on him, how the people did not learn to take care of themselves. Ash wondered if this all had to do with Lysandre Labs. The scientists' early work at the labs had been helpful. They had tried to make machines and other things to do good in the world. It was exactly why Mairin had trusted them to care for her Chespie.

"But it would only be a matter of time before those people would destroy the world with their own need and entitlement," Lysandre claimed. "That's why I am going to create a new world: my utopian dream! But that dream has no room for you!" His words rang out over the wrecked city.

Meanwhile, at the foot of Prism Tower, Clemont and Clembot had finally managed to defeat the Team Flare scientists who had been guarding the entrance. The evil red ray that had taken control of and changed the Squishy Zygarde had come from the Gym. Clemont had to get inside. He tried punching in his Gym code at the front door, but it didn't work.

"It appears the lock code has been changed," he said.

"I can handle this!" Clembot said, plugging into the keypad. Clembot was the substitute Gym Leader Clemont had created. Once they made it in, they saw an immense machine with a supersize laser beam. "I detect the same elements in this device as in the red Zygarde."

"Maybe it's their control system," Clemont said. That machine was terrible. Clemont knew

what he needed to do to help defeat Team Flare:
he had to destroy the machine.

"It is possible that I could infiltrate their
system and stop it from functioning," suggested
Clembot.

"Good!" declared Clemont, and they got
to work.

CHAPTER 5

On the other side of the city, Mairin, Serena, and Professor Sycamore were approaching Lysandre Labs. Their mission was to reclaim Chespie. They were in a helicopter, and Team Rocket was at the controls.

Team Rocket?! Yes, the members of Team Rocket were disguised as a news team, and Meowth and James were in the cockpit.

Professor Sycamore and the young Trainers did not realize it, but Lysandre Labs was also the secret base of Team Flare. Team Rocket had an intense rivalry with Team Flare, so they had willingly volunteered to help our young heroes.

Lysandre Labs was built into the side of a mountain. There were security cameras everywhere. It was clear that Team Flare did not want visitors! A Team Flare scientist named Mable began to attack the news helicopter before it had even landed.

"Weavile, use Ice Shard!" she called. Then Serena directed Braixen to use Flamethrower to counter the Ice Shard. Professor Sycamore worried that their attempt to rescue Chespie would be over before it had even started.

Just in time, Steven Stone—the Hoenn Champion—appeared! He was riding on the back of his Mega Metagross. Steven announced his arrival with one Meteor Mash move, and then he and Mable sparred with words. Steven

accused Team Flare and Lysandre of not being honest about their true mission.

"Oh, please! Deception doesn't have anything to do with it," Mable replied. "The smart thing to do would be to side with us." Some more Team Flare minions appeared, Poké Balls in hand, to back her up.

While Steven distracted Team Flare, Professor Sycamore and the others were able to race inside. Team Rocket, still dressed as a news team, joined them. The group did not get far before more members of Team Flare showed up and blocked one of the lab's long hallways. Team Flare's Drapion sent out a warning Sludge Bomb. The Poison-type move hit the disguised Team Rocket the hardest.

"Are you all right?" Serena asked them. She still did not know their true identity.

Luckily, they were. Making a grand scene, Team Rocket shed their disguises and revealed who they really were: Jessie, James, Meowth, and Wobbuffet!

Although Serena and the others were

surprised by this turn of events, they had bigger issues at hand—plus, when Team Rocket and Team Flare exchanged nasty insults, it was easy to see whose side Team Rocket was on.

"Any enemy of our enemy is a good buddy to us," Meowth claimed.

And then Team Rocket fought off Team Flare while the others went in search of Chespie.

As Mairin, Serena, and Professor Sycamore turned down another of the laboratory's long hallways, they heard the booms of Seed Bomb and Psybeam and Sludge Bomb attacks behind them.

"We'd better hurry!" Professor Sycamore yelled. He hoped they would be able to find

Mairin's Chespie before anyone else from Team Flare found them.

And they did. "Thank goodness!" Mairin said, her voice full of hope. "Chespie is safe." She hadn't known whether she would find her beloved Pokémon there, at Lysandre Labs. But even though Chespie was still sleeping, she could see with her own eyes that it really was safe.

"Let's take Chespie back to my lab," suggested Professor Sycamore, who noticed that Chespie's body glowed with an odd, pale green light. The little Pokémon didn't move when the professor picked it up.

They met Serena in the hall, and Steven

joined them to help fend off any guards as they tried to find a way out of Lysandre Labs. When they got back to the main entrance, they found that Team Rocket had successfully knocked out Mable and her minions. With the pesky guards out of the way, Steven decided to investigate a little in the main lab.

*   *   *

Back in the city, Bonnie had struggles of her own. She had convinced Blaziken Mask that she could appeal to Squishy, that she could break Team Flare's source of control. Blaziken Mask had agreed to let her give it a try, but only if he and Mega Blaziken could stand watch close by.

"Are you sure about this?" Blaziken Mask asked again, needing to know that Bonnie understood there was great danger involved.

"I promised I wouldn't let Squishy go ever, ever again. I know Squishy will understand! Please believe me!" Bonnie begged. She turned to Squishy Zygarde, with its blazing red eyes and deep growl. Bonnie truly believed that

her dear friend would somehow still hear her. "Squishy, it's fine now. It's me, Bonnie!" She paused, searching for some understanding. "Squishy, you don't want to do this, do you?"

Zygarde roared.

Bonnie gasped. She was terrified, but she had to believe in her friend. She thought back to safe feelings, to feelings of togetherness. She thought back to a special moment she and Squishy had shared.

"Squishy, Squishy," Bonnie began to sing softly. "You're oh-so-very soft. Squishy, Squishy, you're oh-so-pretty green." Bonnie sniffed as tears ran down her face. "You're the cutest thing to be I've ever seen."

Bonnie sobbed a little in between verses of the lullaby that she had sung so many times, but she continued to sing. Zygarde continued to growl, but not as loudly as before.

"Squishy, Squishy . . ." Bonnie sang the chorus again, and Zygarde slowly crept closer. "Squishy, how I wish I understood where you come from." Bonnie's voice grew stronger as she looked up at Zygarde. "And the way you get your food from the sun. Mysterious Squishy, how I love you so." Tears ran down Bonnie's cheeks, but she kept singing.

Blaziken Mask rushed down and held Bonnie. In his arms, Bonnie felt safe, so she slowly reached out to Zygarde. Her hand touched its nose.

"Oh Squishy, here's my song for you. Best friends forever, we're so happy." As Bonnie's voice grew in strength, a bizarre, bright globe of light floated near Zygarde's head.

"Little Squishy, I'll never leave, my sweet Squishy, that's you!"

Blasts of energy surged all around. Blaziken Mask tried to shield Bonnie as the dust cleared.

"Squishy," Bonnie whispered, looking up at the giant Legendary Pokémon. "You heard my voice!" The red parts of Squishy Zygarde turned green as the Pokémon bent down close to Bonnie's face. Bonnie hugged its giant nose, and then green sparks began to shoot from all around Squishy Zygarde as the area glowed an intense green.

CHAPTER 6

Even from the top of Prism Tower, it was obvious that there had been a change in Squishy Zygarde. "What's happening?" Ash wondered aloud.

Lysandre scowled as he watched. A bright light glowed around the Zygarde. Lysandre spoke into his Team Flare communicator. "What's going on, Xerosic?" he barked.

"Look, I'm busy," Xerosic replied over the communicator. "I'm battling an intruder in the Gym."

"Battling an intruder?" Lysandre repeated with disgust.

"It's the Lumiose Gym Leader," Xerosic explained.

"Clemont!" Ash said with a gasp of hope.

"You're all so useless," snarled Lysandre.

Suddenly, they all saw the Squishy Zygarde begin to shrink smaller and smaller. In fact, it was not only shrinking, but transforming. In a short time, it was once again tiny Squishy, soft and oh-so-pretty green. Squishy floated over and rested in Bonnie's arms.

"Squishy, you're okay now," Bonnie said. She was so relieved to be back with her friend.

*   *   *

Lysandre had started battling Ash and Alain and their loyal Pokémon, spouting about his world vision and professing his knowledge of Pokémon all the while. His Mega Gyarados aimed attack after attack and showed no sign of weakness. "This power of Mega Evolution only happens during battle," Lysandre declared, motioning to Mega Gyarados. "It's a kind of battle instinct. Something Pokémon forget after being in constant contact with humans. But when a Pokémon unleashes its battle instinct, that's when it gains Mega Evolution power!"

"Stop it!" Alain demanded. "You've got it all wrong."

"Only the victor can prove that he's not wrong, Alain," Lysandre chided, and they began to make steady strikes again.

Mega Gyarados was relentless and strong. Before long, Ash had returned Noivern, Hawlucha, and Goodra to their Poké Balls. Ash knew that they had all given their best fight. It was daunting.

"Oh, done so soon?" Lysandre said, taunting Ash.

"No way! I never quit until it's over!" Ash was not going to give up or give in! "I think

you called that 'fighting spirit.' But there's a lot more to a Pokémon's strength than that! I learned that on my journey. My Pokémon's strength and my strength come from believing in one another and caring for one another more than anything else."

Alain heard what Ash said, and he stood by his friend. He was more committed than ever to fight by Ash's side.

"And if you don't understand *that*," Ash said, "we'll show you!" Ash's remaining Pokémon raised their heads and looked ready—and proud—to fight alongside him.

"Talonflame, now! Use Flame Charge! And Greninja, you use Cut!" Ash's Pokémon charged forward.

Lysandre countered with Mega Gyarados. "Use Stone Edge!" he cried. Mega Gyarados roared, and blue pillars of rock erupted from the ground and rushed at Talonflame and Greninja, knocking them down.

Alain sent Mega Charizard X into the air to cut off Mega Gyarados, but Lysandre called for Dragon Tail. As Mega Gyarados swooped down, its tail lit up with a bright green glow. Mega Gyarados flipped in the air and smacked Mega Charizard X with its tail.

Ash's and Alain's Pokémon were stunned by Lysandre's moves, but it was Talonflame who had taken the worst of the attacks.

"You were great, Talonflame," Ash announced with gratitude, calling it back to a Poké Ball. He took a deep breath.

"What's wrong?" Lysandre asked, faking concern. "Ash, with all that big talk of yours, is that all you can come up with? Well then, this is it! Use Hyper Beam!"

Mega Gyarados unleashed a Hyper Beam move before Ash and Alain could react. They watched as the blast came straight at them . . . but then another, unexpected attack streaked by them and cut off the Hyper Beam.

"Time for all this to end," a voice announced from behind Ash and Alain. "Right now!"

"Malva," Alain gasped. He had not seen that Team Flare member for a while.

"Malva," Lysandre repeated with surprise. "What is the meaning of all this?"

"It's really simple," Malva said, striding up to where Alain and Ash stood. "I'm putting my

complete trust in these kids. I know this world is hardly perfect. Far from it."

"Then why are you getting in my way?" Lysandre asked, disgusted.

"Because I saw *them*," Malva answered. "Changing the world isn't about destroying it! And people like them are proof of that!"

"Then let me ask you. These children, who are destined to lose—what kind of world are they capable of making?" Lysandre demanded.

"They haven't lost yet, have they?" Malva pointed out. She gave a sly smile. She stared Lysandre down from behind her orchid-tinted glasses. It was clear she no longer believed in

Team Flare's mission. "Changing the world is not something these kids can do themselves, but if adults like us offer to lend a hand, then I'm sure things can change for the better. The possibilities are real, and I want to see them." Malva stood her ground, surrounded by Ash, Alain, and their crew of Pokémon.

"Our conversation is through," Lysandre blurted, feeling betrayed. The droids buzzed above him, and his goggles blazed a bright orange. "You've wasted enough of my precious time! Gyarados, Incinerate, NOW!"

Ash had been listening closely. He was surprised to hear Malva say what she did. Her words gave him hope, and they gave him strength. He believed he and Alain could beat Lysandre, and he knew they had something to teach him. "Greninja! Water Shuriken!" Ash yelled, calling on their special Ash-Greninja Bond Phenomenon move.

Then Ash addressed Lysandre. "Now look!" he yelled. "You may not like this world

much—so what? It belongs to people and Pokémon. Everyone! Your plan to re-create the world . . . All that talk . . . You have no right to say any of that! The world is full of possibilities! There are people meeting new people all the time. People making their dreams come true. People just getting started on their journeys, and people healing from old wounds. Everyone's got their own tomorrow, and you have no right to take their tomorrows away from them!" Ash took another deep breath. He thought of all his friends and how each and every one was waging a battle today. "That's why we fight. My Pokémon and I are fighting for their tomorrows!"

"Sounds like the future Ash talks about is pretty bright," Malva commented.

"How naïve can you get? You sound just like me back in the days when *I* was naïve!" Lysandre scoffed. He raised his arm and aimed it at Malva, Ash, and Alain. "Use Hyper Beam!"

"Pikachu, use Quick Attack!" Ash commanded. Pikachu made a good hit.

"Keep up the heat!" Alain said to Mega Charizard X. "Use Dragon Claw!"

"Greninja, use Cut now!" Ash called.

The two Pokémon rose into the air and unleashed their moves from above. With both attacks making contact, Mega Gyarados shrunk back in pain.

"Pikachu, use Thunderbolt!"

"Pika-chuuuuuu!" Pikachu drew energy from deep within and aimed a giant bolt right at Gyarados's giant, gaping maw. Gyarados fell to the ground.

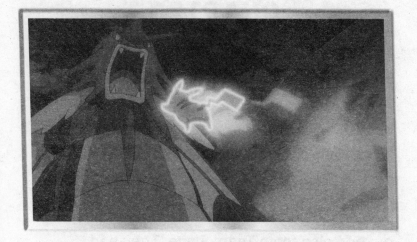

"It appears that the fighting instinct you've spoken of is a thing of the past," said Alain, putting Lysandre in his place.

"It's all over, Lysandre," Ash stated.

Lysandre returned Gyarados to its Poké ball. "All your petty talk," he replied, steadily backing away, "it will never extinguish my dream. I'm still committed to re-creating this world." He stopped at the edge of the tower. He reached his arms wide, and he fell backward.

"Greninja!" Ash yelled, hoping it might catch Lysandre, but by the time the group rushed to the edge, Lysandre was gone.

They stood in silence, not knowing what to think.

CHAPTER 7

"What are you doing?" Serena asked Steven as she glanced around for anyone else from Team Flare. They had rescued Chespie, and Serena wasn't sure why they were still there. It seemed dangerous.

"I'm finding out what kind of research was being conducted here," Steven answered.

The lab was full of countless machines and devices. But the most interesting thing was in the very center. It was a gigantic rock enclosed in an enormous glass case. It looked like the scientists had been doing tests on it. It glowed with an intense red energy.

Steven looked at the data on the giant screen and frowned. "There it is," he said at last.

Serena and Mairin stepped a little closer to take a look.

All at once, the rock glowed even brighter, and the lab was filled with a buzzing sound. "What is it?" Professor Sycamore asked.

Then, with a crash, the enormous glass case burst and the lab filled with smoke.

"Chespie?" Mairin said, struggling to keep hold of the Pokémon in her arms. "Hey!"

An invisible force pulled Chespie from Mairin's grasp and carried it, through the air, toward the Giant Rock.

"Chespie!" Mairin screamed.

"Mairin, wait!" Professor Sycamore warned.

"But Chespie disappeared," Mairin said. She couldn't believe that she had lost her Chespie—again!

"We've got to get away, Mairin," Professor Sycamore said as the ceiling began to crumble around them. Once they were all safely outside, they looked back. The mountainside that had been the entrance to Lysandre Labs began to fall away in large chunks of red rock. From the rubble, the Giant Rock that had been in the main lab emerged. It was moving on its own! There was a glowing red dot at its center, and vinelike tentacles stretched out from all sides.

"Professor Sycamore, what's happening?" Serena asked.

"I have no idea," the professor admitted. "Is the Giant Rock involved?"

"Involved?" repeated Steven. "I'm certain the Giant Rock is the source. Anything can happen now."

As the Giant Rock began to crawl away from the mountain, it let out a ferocious roar. But all Mairin could think was that her Chespie was deep inside.

*   *   *

While Bonnie and Blaziken Mask were confronting Squishy Zygarde, Clemont and Clembot had managed to override the computer system of the evil machine that controlled the first Zygarde. Unfortunately, Clembot had to be connected to the machine's computer system in order to cancel Team Flare's coding—and when Clemont shut down the system, it wiped out Clembot's memory. It was the only way to stop Lysandre's control of the Legendary Zygarde.

As soon as Clemont cut the machine's power, the red-and-black Zygarde had changed back to its Core form.

Now, Bonnie followed little Squishy as it bounced through the dust and rubble, searching for what was left of the other Zygarde. They soon found it in its Core form.

"Yay!" Bonnie said, and kneeled down to speak to the Core. It looked just like Squishy, except the pink hexagons that appeared on Squishy were blue on the other Core. "Hello

there," she said kindly. "I'm good friends with Squishy."

But the Zygarde Core backed away from Bonnie.

Squishy was determined to get through to the Core, but it was full of anger and distrust.

Because they were both forms of Zygarde, the Core was able to speak with Squishy through telepathy—they could read each other's thoughts. *Look at this devastation!* it said. *Humans did this. This is why they're so . . . evil!*

Squishy was quick to share its thoughts, too. *I believe in humans.*

How can you say such a thing? the Core wondered.

Because these humans haven't given up yet, Squishy replied. *Being on a journey with this girl and her friends has allowed me to witness many things. They help one another. They work hard. They share their happiness together. They trust one another, and they never give up! That's how the humans I travel with are.*

Bonnie tried again to persuade the Core. "Oh

please, come here," she said. "Don't be scared. Why don't you come with us?"

The Core made a few muffled squeaks, but it did not seem to change its opinion of humans at all.

"If Squishy's a friend of yours, then I'm your friend, too!" Bonnie said good-heartedly. She reached out. "I won't hurt you. I want to be your friend." When the Core did not move, Bonnie scooped it up in her hands. "Okay," she said, "when I tickle Squishy under the chin like this, then it laughs." Bonnie proceeded to tickle the Core, and it let out a string of muffled, frustrated chirps. Then it appeared to pass out.

*　　*　　*

As all the friends tried to regroup and figure out what do to next, Professor Sycamore and the others who had rescued Chespie shared an update. The biggest news was that the Giant Rock that had been in Lysandre Labs was now mysteriously on the move. While they tracked the rock in an airplane, the professor and Steven contacted Ash and his team.

"When we scanned the rock, we discovered that it is a giant mass of energy," Professor Sycamore explained. "A mass of energy that strongly resembles Zygarde's." Of course, no one really understood what that meant. "In addition, we were able to pick up Chespie's vital signs from within the rock's core."

Ash and Alain sighed with relief. If they were able to hear Chespie's heartbeat in the rock, then maybe they would be able to save it. For her part, Mairin had been very brave. It helped to have someone like Serena by her side. The young Pokémon Trainers listened closely as

Professor Sycamore and Steven shared everything they had learned.

"We found Chespie's records in the lab's database," Steven added. "According to the records, there was an accident where Chespie absorbed some of Zygarde's energy. We think the Giant Rock absorbed Chespie in order to get that energy."

Ash had not realized how much Mega Evolution and Zygarde energy were at the root of all this turmoil. It was all very confusing.

"Now that the Giant Rock is on the move, it is probably in search of its next energy source," Professor Sycamore added solemnly. He shared the graphic from their screen with Ash and the others, who were flying with Malva in a helicopter. The graphic scanned the area where the Giant Rock was headed. In the distance, they all saw a well-known landmark.

"Isn't that . . ." Alain began.

"It's Anistar City!" Professor Sycamore exclaimed. Everyone gasped.

"It's headed for the sundial," Steven stated.

"The sundial is a giant crystal said to have come from space. We know that the energy it contains is the very same energy that Pokémon emit when experiencing Mega Evolution."

But when the team discussed why the Giant Rock might be drawn to the sundial's energy, the realization was terrifying. "I know why," Professor Sycamore stated, his voice grave. "If the Giant Rock and the sundial come in direct contact and then merge . . ." He paused, not knowing how to say it. "If they come together, it's the end of the world."

"It's Lysandre, re-creating the world at any

cost!" Alain declared. He slammed his fist against the helicopter wall.

"We won't let that happen," said Ash. "Professor, we've gotta rescue Chespie and stop that rock right away!"

"Okay, we're with you," Serena replied.

The two groups signed off so they could prepare for the next stage of their fight. They needed to warn people near the sundial. And they needed to reach out to others who might be able to assist them in the coming battle.

The Giant Rock continued toward Anistar, leaving a cloud of thick dust behind. It was the size of a house and seemed to hover just above the ground. It no longer looked like an enormous rock. It had sprouted large tentacles much like the vines Zygarde had used to trash the city of Lumiose. The tentacles slithered in the air as the Giant Rock barreled along— drawn toward the energy of the sundial.

CHAPTER 8

With Malva at the helm, the helicopter carrying Ash, Clemont, and many of our other heroes caught up with the team who was trailing the rock.

Watching the Giant Rock from above, Ash and Clemont knew they needed a plan. "Professor, do you know Chespie's exact location?" Clemont asked over the helicopter's radio.

"The scan shows Chespie is somewhere in its core," the professor answered.

Ash and his Greninja were already sharing Bond Phenomenon. They both stared into the fiery center of the Giant Rock. Deep in the burning core, they sensed something. Ash gasped. "Did you see it, too?" he whispered. Ash-Greninja did.

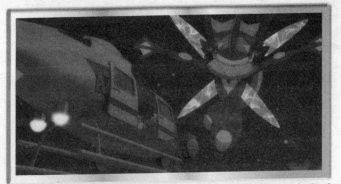

With that, they devised a plan. Ash-Greninja had a clear mission, and it had a full support team as well. It dived out of the helicopter toward the rock.

"Make sure you've got Greninja's back, Pikachu!" Ash called.

"Pika!" Pikachu called from its perch on Mega Charizard X's back.

"Let's help Ash all we can," Professor Sycamore agreed. Mega Metagross and Mega Garchomp were also ready to do their part.

The crew of Pokémon flew straight toward the Giant Rock's core.

"Chespie, take care," Mairin whispered from the plane. "And be safe."

From the helicopter, Bonnie was also watching and hoping for the best. In her lap, both tiny Zygarde Cores were intent on the battle at hand.

"There it is!" Ash cried. The Bond Phenomenon allowed him to visualize in his mind what Ash-Greninja was seeing with its eyes. "Greninja, use Water Shuriken. Now!"

Ash-Greninja aimed a Water Shuriken, and it sliced deep into the Giant Rock's core where the sleeping Chespie was trapped.

Now their target was clear. Everyone knew where to focus their energy. If they all aimed for Ash-Greninja's Water Shuriken, they could get Chespie out.

But no number of Flamethrower, Thunder

Bolt, Flash Cannon, and Hyper Beam moves could overwhelm the Giant Rock. Its tentacles snatched at the Pokémon and cinched them tightly.

"It's endless," Steven said in dismay.

"At this rate, we won't be able to get close," Professor Sycamore agreed.

"Quick, use Cut!" Ash called, but it was no use. Soon, all the Pokémon were bound by the greedy vines. They struggled and squirmed, but the tentacles only gripped them harder.

"I don't like this one bit!" Jessie pouted in the news helicopter. The rest of Team Rocket was silent with concern.

Then, a huge pulse of energy streaked through the sky and hit the Giant Rock, releasing the Pokémon. The Giant Rock sputtered to a stop.

Everyone was incredibly relieved, and when they realized the source of the pulse, they were delighted.

"Look at all the Gym Leaders!" Clemont cheered.

A large group had gathered, and when the helicopter landed near them, Ash could hardly believe who it was. There were Gym Leaders of all ages, who specialized in different kinds of Pokémon. Trainers from all over the Kalos region. Seeing them, Ash realized what an amazing journey he was on, filled with generous, talented, and kind people who took incredible pride in their own Pokémon journeys.

"Yippee! Yay!" Bonnie called.

"Sorry to keep you waiting," Diantha replied. Her elegant Mega Gardevoir was by her side.

Viola, Grant, and Ramos all commented on the giant size of their opponent.

"Horrendous energy is everywhere," said Valerie, the Fairy-type Pokémon specialist.

"It must not make contact with the sundial," Olympia warned. The starry night-sky pattern of her cape flapped in the wind.

The Giant Rock, with its massive plantlike tentacles, began to plow ahead again.

Diantha was shocked. "Our attack didn't even slow it down," she said. "Let's fall back and come up with a different plan."

The Trainers and Champions and Gym Leaders and their Pokémon all took a moment to catch their breath . . . and catch up. Malva and Houndoom. Ramos and Gogoat. Wulfric and Mega Abomasnow. Viola and Vivillon. Korrina and Mega Lucario. There were so many strong teams uniting in the fight.

"So this is the famous Greninja?" said Korrina, the Shalour City Gym Leader.

"Sure is," Ash said with pride. "Its power merges with mine!"

"Excellent!" Korrina replied.

"And now you have finally made that power yours," Olympia congratulated Ash.

Diantha and Steven discussed various plans. As the Giant Rock roared closer, they turned to the group. "We all know rescuing Chespie is our first priority," Diantha reminded everyone.

"Right," Steven agreed. "Let's use the Pokémon's moves to get into the Giant Rock." He pointed to the Water Shuriken as the target.

"Everyone! You're looking at the final line of defense!" Diantha rallied them. "We cannot let it come in contact with the sundial. Remember that at all times."

Ash, Clemont, and Alain took a special moment with Serena, Bonnie, and Mairin. Alain reassured Mairin that he wouldn't give up until Chespie was safe back in her arms. Squishy and the other Zygarde Core listened as the friends wished one another luck.

"Now, you all be careful," Bonnie said.

Team Rocket took in the moment as well. "Viewers of the world, this is history!" Jessie announced, looking straight into the camera as they broadcast like an actual news team. "Watch as these titans tackle the threat to Kalos . . . and the world!"

This amazing gathering of Pokémon and Trainers prepared for the battle of a lifetime.

"Everybody, head toward the Water Shuriken!" Diantha directed as they all took off running. "That's where Chespie is! We must save Chespie first!"

The Pokémon and Trainers were all in from the start, but the viny tentacles of the Giant Rock were everywhere. They wove themselves into blockades. They separated Trainers from Pokémon. And they knocked everyone down, whether on the ground or in the sky.

"Pikachu, use Iron Tail!" Ash yelled.

Pikachu rose up and performed the move. *"Pi-ka!"*

Alain, Malva, and Blaziken Mask all called for Flamethrower at once, burning different parts of the greedy vines, but the damage did not last long.

The Pokémon attacks had little effect on the thick hide of the vines. As the Trainers got closer to the core, the viny tentacles were so thick that they could run on them. Each time a vine moved, it sounded like a villainous growl.

While Ash, Ash-Greninja, and Alain neared the core, the others worked to protect them.

When Valerie was nabbed by a vine, Olympia directed Ash and Alain to keep moving. "I'll help out here. Save that Chespie!" The heroes ducked under and leaped over grasping vines. When they saw Korrina and Mega Lucario locked in battle against the rock, Korrina yelled, "You guys need to turn around and run!"

"Got it," Ash grunted. "Thank you." They rushed past as Viola, Grant, Wulfric, and their Pokémon were waging attacks. "Hurry up, young ones," Wulfric yelled. Malva, Professor Sycamore, Diantha, and Clemont secured a path, so Ash and Alain could reach the core . . . and eventually Chespie.

"Dark Pulse, go!"

"Mega Garchomp, use Dragon Rage!"

"Bunnelby, use Mud Shot!"

It went against Ash's every belief to run past his friends while they were struggling in battle, but he and Alain had to be true to their mission.

"Pika, pika, pika!" Pikachu was using Iron Tail over and over.

"We won't let you down," Ash murmured as he ran toward the rock's core. Pokémon attacks of

all kinds zapped and blasted and sizzled in every direction, but the vines kept coming.

Serena, Mairin, and Bonnie watched as the Giant Rock rumbled ahead, churning up a wall of dust.

From the safety of Bonnie's arms, the Zygarde Cores watched, too. *Why are they giving so much?* the Core asked Squishy, using telepathy.

I've realized from observing them that this is how people and Pokémon really are, Squishy responded. *They truly care.*

Even Team Rocket joined the clash, blasting at the Giant Rock to protect Alain and Ash.

"Don't worry about the vines!" Steven reminded them.

"Keep moving forward," Diantha demanded. "Our future depends on it!"

"Over there!" Ash yelled. He pointed to where he had glimpsed a sliver of the Water Shuriken deep inside the core of the Giant Rock. "Pikachu, Electro Ball! Greninja, Water Shuriken!"

"Charizard, Flamethrower!" Alain called up to Mega Charizard X.

"Let's go!" With all the Kalos Gym Leaders and two Champions calling out battle cries and distracting the Giant Rock, Ash and Alain entered the core.

Inside, it was oddly quiet.

"Chespie, Hang on!" Alain cried.

"I'll cover you as best I can, Alain. Now you go and get Chespie!" Ash said. As soon as Alain charged off, Ash started his defense. "Charizard, help me out!"

Mega Charizard X, Pikachu, and Ash-Greninja launched a flurry of their best moves, following Ash's game plan. Flamethrower!

Electro Ball! Cut! The Giant Rock groaned with rage. The Pokémon attacks held off the burning shards of rock that were aimed at Alain. Again and again, the Pokémon deflected the Giant Rock's strikes on him.

"Chespie, it's Alain. I've come to get you out of here," Alain called to the trapped Pokémon, who appeared to still be sleeping. "Let's go back to Mairin together." Then Alain leaped toward Chespie as the core seemed to collapse around him.

The next thing Alain knew, everything was still. Then he was riding Mega Charizard X out of the core with Chespie in his arms. Ash, Ash-Greninja, and Pikachu were escaping, too.

Reuniting Chespie and Mairin was cause for celebration.

"Chespie, I've got you," Mairin exclaimed and hugged the Pokémon. "Thank you so much!" She looked up at Alain and wept with joy.

*　　*　　*

Everyone, humans and Pokémon alike, knew that rescuing Chespie was only the first part of their mission. They needed to recognize the good effort of all. But they could not stop there.

"All that's left is what is in front of us," Steven said, looking to the Giant Rock. It was motionless as it loomed over them.

"Let's all attack together!" Diantha directed. "Now!"

Every Pokémon and Trainer focused all their energy on the Giant Rock. A charge of every color and kind blasted the mysterious rock. Once the blitz was over, there was momentary silence.

"Did it work?" asked Ash.

But then the Giant Rock roared like never before, shaking everything for miles, and a figure appeared, balanced on top of the monstrous creation.

"It can't be," Alain said with a gasp.

"I know," said Ash. "But how?"

"Lysandre," Malva stated.

"Time is almost up," Lysandre declared. "Even if you're somehow able to stop me, I will *still* destroy the world. Count on it." Lysandre was wearing his blazing orange goggles and his mechanical jetpack. The flying droids buzzed around his head, and he wore the weaponized cuffs on his wrists.

"How is he doing this?" Ash wondered aloud. How did he gain so much power?

"The countdown to destruction will not stop!" Lysandre bellowed.

"Here it comes!" Diantha called out a warning. Valerie and Spritzee put up a protective force field just in time. Lysandre's huge attack blasted around them.

"Such power!" James yelped, ducking against the rush of the ambush.

"Will this insanity never end?" Jessie wondered out loud.

The team of heroes paused to check on one another, all taking refuge under the force field. Ash reached out for Pikachu and Greninja. Alain made sure Mega Charizard X was safe.

Clemont and Bonnie crawled out from under the protection of Blaziken Mask's cape only to discover that the secret identity of the masked hero was their own father. "Dad?" they said together.

"Guilty as charged," their masked dad said, hugging both of them.

"You all right?" Bonnie asked with concern.

"Don't worry. I'm just fine," he said, bending down to see them better. "You two?"

The Zygarde Cores both shook off the dust from the blast and watched the humans and Pokémon regroup.

CHAPTER 10

"The Giant Rock is moving," Diantha warned. The ground began to vibrate as it approached.

"Everyone, listen to me!" Clemont said. "The power has something to do with the device on Lysandre's arm!"

Ash remembered the device from their showdown on top of Prism Tower. It controlled Lysandre's Mega Gyarados, and now it seemed to control the Giant Rock's power, too. The Giant Rock heaved as it plowed over everything in its way. It soon would catch up to them, and then it would reach the sundial. And then . . .

"The device must be destroyed NOW!" Alain insisted.

"That will stop it?" questioned Ash.

"We have to try," Diantha said. "We have to give it everything we have left. It's our only chance!"

The heroes all lined up again, prepared to fight until they had no fight left.

The Zygarde Core was confused. It looked to its Squishy counterpart. *So they will fight?* it asked with awe. *Against that tremendous evil?*

Neither humans nor Pokémon give up, Squishy replied.

But they are far too weak!

None of them think they are weak! Squishy said. *It's true that humans are weak and powerless. But they have dreams, and they believe in one another. They stand together and feel empathy for one another! That is their real strength. They have the power to believe in themselves, and within themselves, they somehow find the will to succeed!* Squishy's voice was full of admiration for humans and Pokémon.

Then I will believe in them! the Zygarde Core decided.

Now you understand, Squishy stated with satisfaction.

The two tiny Zygarde Cores hurried away and took a stand, facing the Giant Rock as it approached.

"Squishy!" Bonnie called, unsure of what was happening.

I am Zygarde—defender of order! the Cores chanted in unison.

From every city and every countryside, zaps of powerful green energy pulsated and streaked across the globe. They came together and grew and grew until they had transformed into something like the Zygarde that had terrorized Lumiose City. But it was

also altogether different, as all the sources of energy had become one. An impressive Forme floated in the air, a warrior worthy of defending order and the whole of the world.

"What's this?" Lysandre scoffed.

"Oh, Squishy!" Bonnie cried, her voice full of pride.

"Is that Zygarde?" Alain asked.

"Those deep green eyes," Olympia noted. "That is it. That is the Forme when all has become one."

"Become one?" Ash repeated in awe.

"And still you hid this Forme?" Lysandre scolded the Legendary Pokémon. "You must have been seeing this world in the same way I

was. The unlimited greed of humans has sent the world spinning into chaos. But NOW you choose to appear? What could possibly be left to defend?" Lysandre's words were full of hate and ire. "You have no right!"

Zygarde Complete floated tall above Lysandre and the Giant Rock. *If it is a right you speak of, this world belongs to them.* Zygarde Complete's telepathic voice boomed for all to hear. *I have placed my hopes in humanity! They have always protected me. They kept their promise not to leave my side. Now it is my turn!*

Lysandre's eyes narrowed. "I will incinerate you!" he screamed. He aimed his fist at Zygarde Complete, and the Giant Rock shot a superpowered blast from its red-hot core.

Four brilliant beams burst from Zygarde Complete and met the blast head-on. At once, Zygarde Complete vaulted into the air and bounded toward the Giant Rock with elegance and speed. It effortlessly slashed the tentacles of the Giant Rock, again and again. Then it bounded back and took aim at the Giant Rock, targeting the glowing red core. A brilliant neon green pulse of energy burned into the core.

"Impudent fool," growled Lysandre.

"All right, Pikachu," Ash said, "use Thunderbolt! Greninja, use Water Shuriken!"

Alain chimed in, directing Mega Charizard X to use Flamethrower.

Following Clemont's advice, the Pokémon aimed for the weaponized bands on Lysandre's arms. The blasts were fast and furious, and Lysandre cried out in agony as the clasps broke open and the damaged bands fell to the ground.

"It can't be! It must be a mistake," Lysandre

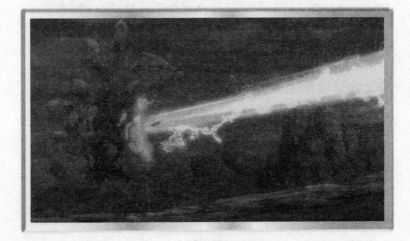

declared, raising his hands in defiance. "All my meticulous planning was perfect!"

Kalos, I will protect you! Zygarde Complete promised, rising into the air.

"Squishy!" Bonnie cheered, watching in amazement. "Squishy, go for it!" Even though Squishy had combined and transformed into the highest Forme of a Legendary Pokémon, Bonnie still felt a connection to it.

Surges of green energy flowed all around Zygarde Complete, churning up a whirlwind. Zygarde sent a beam that etched out the letter "Z" in the ground, and the earth rumbled. Energy seemed to come from deep in

the ground, from the tallest mountaintop, and it whipped all around. The Trainers and Pokémon braced against the steady force. The energy was so strong, so bright, some of them had to look away. When the energy came to a rest again, Lysandre was gone.

"That is a wrap!" Meowth announced.

"Look!" James said, his typical confidence returning. "Look at what we did, world!"

"That giant monstrosity is gone, but we're still standing!" Jessie bragged. Team Rocket had survived! And so had their triumphant attitudes.

"The sundial was protected," Olympia informed the happy crowd.

"Thank you, everyone," Diantha said with great gratitude.

"We won, we really won!" Korrina cheered.

There were questions about where Lysandre had gone, but no one could be sure. Malva assured the Gym Leaders that she would take responsibility for Team Flare.

Mairin had been quietly content when she looked down to an unfamiliar sight. Chespie's eyes were fluttering open. "Chespie, you're awake," she whispered. "You're awake!" she repeated, hugging the Pokémon with all her might. She hurried to tell Alain the happy news.

Alain shared Mairin's joy, and then he turned serious. "Mairin, please forgive me," he said. "For everything I did."

"Stop," Mairin said, knowing that Alain had only aligned himself with Lysandre in hopes of helping her and Chespie. "I'm just happy you're all right."

Another pair was reunited, too. "Squishy! Thanks a lot!" Bonnie said, looking up at Zygarde Complete.

Bonnie, I only did what you have done for

me all along. It is I who should thank you. I'm so grateful, Zygarde Complete said. Then it began to slowly transform again. Green ripples radiated all around as Zygarde Complete became two tiny green Cores once again. The glowing Cores floated in the dark night sky.

"Che-pii!" Chespie called out. *"Che-pii!"*

It's you! Squishy said upon seeing Chespie. Squishy realized now the role that Chespie had played. It was Chespie who had first rescued Squishy in Lysandre Labs, even before Squishy met Bonnie. Lysandre had already been trying to harness Zygarde's power. Thanks to Chespie, Squishy had been able to escape. But during that rescue, Chespie had an accident. And that's

how Chespie ended up with part of Zygarde's power—and why the Giant Rock had then absorbed Chespie.

Mairin and Chespie were both shocked. Squishy's gratitude was genuine. Then, the Zygarde Core turned back to Bonnie. *Bonnie, to have journeyed with you, and to have learned about humans from you, I am grateful.*

Bonnie swallowed back tears. "Is this good-bye?" she asked.

I'm tired. I think I'd like to rest in the sun. I'm glad to have met you, Squishy said.

"Oh, Squishy, I'm glad to have met you, too!" Bonnie said.

I'll never forget you, the Zygarde Core assured her.

"I love you, Squishy!" Bonnie said. "I love you!" She waved good-bye to her dear friend. All the heroic Pokémon and the Kalos Champions and Gym Leaders watched as the protector of order disappeared into the starry sky.

And so, the final curtain fell on Team Flare and their villainous threat to the Kalos region. The sun will rise again on the world that Ash and his friends worked so hard to protect— the world where they saw hope and promise and where they believed people could make a difference. A world full of tomorrows.

And now, for Ash and his team, the journey continues!